Two Dogs In Africa

By

DJ Cowdall

http://www.davidcowdall.com
https://twitter.com/djcowdall
https://www.facebook.com/DJCowdall

Other Works By DJ Cowdall

Novels

The Dog Under The Bed

I Was A Teenage Necromancer

I Was A Teenage Necromancer: Supernature. Part One

The Magic Christmas Tree

The Kids of Pirate Island

53%: Book One.

Hypnofear

Short Stories

Inferno

Kites

Sacrifice

A Breath of Magic

Available from all good booksellers

CHAPTER ONE

Being just fourteen years old, and called in to ask if you want to go and live in Africa, you can imagine the surprise on my face and how I reacted. Disbelief was the first thing, that it would never happen, and even if it did, would I want to go?

The first thing my father told me after suggesting it, was not to tell anyone, because it wasn't a sure thing. Naturally I went outside, met all my friends from around where I lived, and told every single one of them all the details. To this date I still have no idea what my mother thought, it seemed nobody bothered to ask her. Such were our lives back then.

It was an odd time to do it, studying exams at school, not long having moved to the North West of the UK, and still settling in, only to hear this news, it was like watching a film where they discover someone in their family has lost their mind and needs to run away. When something apparently absurd happens to you, you just go along with it.

Still, being so young, and considering the idea that opting out of school might be a possibility, I figured I wanted to go. Of course at that age you never think about the consequences on your life, only how good it can be. You are after all, immortal at that age.

Time passed quickly then, like a blur, where all I could recall was telling everyone who would listen that we were leaving, going to live in Africa. I left school thinking nothing of it, until like an oncoming car crash, it hit us at full speed as we packed to leave, me, mum and dad. Sister didn't want to go; such a fool!

I felt like a lost sheep, being dragged along back to its pen, having no say where I was going or what I was doing. Firstly we got a plane to Amsterdam, which then took us on a Boeing 747 to Nairobi, Kenya. My dad had shown it to me on a map and had some books about it, with pictures. It would definitely make for an exciting holiday! Because that is how I saw it: a holiday. It didn't sink in that we weren't just going for two weeks then home again. By the time it did sink in, it was too late.

Still, going to Holland was fun, even if that was only a stop off for a few hours, and then being on such a huge plane for so long, crossing the Equator, that was fun. By the time we arrived in Kenya, around twelve hours later, I was exhausted. We got picked up, and driven the my dad's new employers, where we chatted as I tried not to slump over and fall asleep.

After a short while they took us to our new home, a small villa in the hills on the outskirts of Nairobi. It was a nice place, with a huge garden. It was a single story bungalow, with black metal bars on the windows, which I thought were to keep the lions out!

What stood out most though was the back garden, which was nice, but beyond the white picket fence was a huge field, with a stream running through it. Back home in England I had often thought it fun to build a small dam in a stream, but it never occurred to me that in Africa it might not be safe to do so. I would have to learn quickly.

Once we settled in, apart from the sun, there wasn't an awful lot to do there. There was only one television channel, which didn't show a great deal, and of course being back in the nineteen eighties the Internet wasn't even a thing, let alone mobile phones or computers. Imagine that!

Reading became a great joy for me, but of course that was interrupted by my having to attend St Mary's school. Fun though, amounted to eating, reading, and kicking a ball. Truth be told, after a very short time there, I became restless, no nearby friends of my age, nothing to enjoy as a teenager, so I struggled to adapt.

One Saturday morning my dad came to me and asked if I was getting up out of bed. It was around eleven in the morning, and I was wondering what to do, if anything. I suspect my parents must have noticed a problem, because I got the shock of my life.

"David, come on, get up. We're thinking of going to get a dog," he said, sounding as if it were just the same as going to a bit of shopping. Obviously I did jump up, it was such a shock and a great idea. Whenever I thought of Africa, if someone mentioned a cat, I would think they meant something bigger than me with claws. I couldn't imagine there were ordinary dogs, because of all the wild animals, insects and snakes, that surely they wouldn't be safe. Again, I was wrong.

"Where can we get a dog from?" I shouted, struggling to put on clothes, walk and talk at the same time. I ended up wearing odd socks, and my t-shirt inside out by the time I got into the living room.

"Someone I work with, he has a dog, and can't look after him as he is moving away. So I said we would go and meet him, and see if he might be nice enough for us to take in."

It wasn't typical of my dad to do such things, so I wasn't going to argue. At the age I was, I never thought how sad it was that someone had to leave a dog behind, for them or the dog. All I could think was we might get a dog, a new pet, someone to play with.

I skipped breakfast, fixed my top, but not my socks and jumped in the car before mum and dad had even gotten ready. My dad was a big man, very tall, and well built. He was a factory manager building furniture. Mum was much shorter, a complete opposite to him, always so kind and gentle, where he was forthright and direct. However they were, back then they made a great team, and with my mother's guidance dad tended to do the right thing.

I admit I felt some apprehension. We weren't getting a puppy, we were getting an old dog, but that's all I knew. It would be a drive of around forty five minutes to the place, on the other side of Nairobi city centre. The roads around the city are really good, and even major roads joining large towns and cities are good. Once you get out of the city or major towns, however, it becomes uneven mud roads and some are very rough.

As always the sun shone, and it was a lovely day and place to be in. I could forget being bored or away from my friends, because I was going to get a dog, and he would become everything to me. Or so I hoped.

We drove for what seemed an age, until we came upon another town. It wasn't at all as I had expected, where I had been used to shops and houses and flats made of brick, we came upon a very uneven, bumpy road, which led to what they called a shanty town. The houses as they were, were made of bits of wood, corrugated iron sheeting and bits of plastic. They are assembled haphazardly, barely keeping draughts and cold out, or heat in. I was shocked I'll admit, that people had to live like it. No matter I thought back then, because they seemed happy, but I think it was a case of having no alternative and just getting on with it.

It became a factor in my life in Kenya, that there was more of a divide in that country than I had ever witnessed before. Modern people talk of divides between people for all kinds of reasons, but seeing the difference between ourselves, living in a brick villa with land, and good money coming in, and these people, living in such poor conditions, no running water, no electric and no guarantee of where the next meal might come from, it certainly made me think. This certainly wasn't what I had expected Africa to be.

No matter what, people there I found fundamentally no different than others in my own country. There were good people and bad people, but mostly everyone just got on with their lives.

It was a Saturday and the sun was very hot. We had no air conditioning in our car, which was old and had been loaned to use by my father's employers. I sat in the back, bouncing around on the fake leather seats, wondering how long it was going to take. In any other circumstances I would have been bored and unhappy at being so hot with little to do. It was only the thought of getting a dog that made me happy and looking forward to getting to our destination.

The road was more like driving on the moon, at times I thought we might tip up. It was all dried mud, but I could imagine how bad it must be when it rained, like a river running through it, a boggy mess impossible to walk or travel on. Either side of the poor road were various shacks, with an occasional small brick building that had Coca Cola signs outside, suggesting it was a shop. I was glad my dad seemed to know where he was going, because I had the feeling we couldn't stop and ask for directions. We didn't speak a word of Swahili, and I didn't think many would speak English.

It struck me how much I had taken for granted in life, such as street lighting. I imagined in the night it would be so dark that passage would be difficult, possibly hazardous. In many western cities and towns, apart from lighting there tends to be the natural light from the city glow. Here all there would be were fires from stoves and torches, if they could afford them.

As we drove down the winding mud road, at the long end I could see a thin man, standing looking out. We wore a bright yellow t-shirt and loose fitting worn blue jeans. He had nothing on his feet, but he was looking directly at us, wearing the widest grin I could ever remember. He seemed delighted to see we were on our way towards him.

"There he is, that's the fella from work," my dad said, trying not to lose control of the car with all the potholes and bumps. Either side of us people of all types milled around, many wearing sublimely colourful clothes, carrying bags, washing, even a man with a newspaper. I was amazed at how busy it was, so many, all apparently organised and working around one another like a well-oiled machine.

We slowed our driving even more, as my dad pulled up to a track which separated from the main road. It led through some trees, which I could see was gated off to prevent us going further.

"Jambo Sana," the man said, as my dad pulled up and stepped out of the car. They took each other's hand and shook warmly, with my dad reciprocating the smile. I wondered how my dad might discuss anything with this man, as none of my family had yet learned anything of the local language, Swahili.

"Jambo," my dad repeated, which was a pleasant surprise, because it was one word more than I had yet bothered to learn. Obviously it was a kind of hello, but it was nice to get to meet face to face with someone who had more on their mind than just work related.

The man turned and looked at my mother, and to me and in perfect English said, "Hello, how are you?"

I gave a brief 'hi' back to him, and mum smiling likewise said hello too. He was just such a cheerful, pleasant man, he left a lasting impression on me, and from time to time while living in Africa, I would often come up against these kinds of people, who appeared so at peace with their lives, very happy to meet us. It seemed an odd contrast in a way to how people would be in my own country, much more reserved. I was left in the end thinking how sad it was that we couldn't all be as open and welcoming as these people. Clearly we had a lot to learn.

"You have come here about the dog?" the man asked, looking at us all in turn.

"Yes, we thought it might be nice to have a dog around, plus someone to protect the place and us a little." My dad replied, putting on that odd posh accent he often did naturally, in an unconscious effort to impress others, I would guess. I always promised myself I wouldn't do something like it, but I guess we can't always control who we are. It was no criticism, but I always wondered how real it was.

The man burst out laughing. It was such a lovely day, so warm and clear and the skies so blue, here he was too so full of joy, it was infectious, and made it a day I will never forget. If I was ever left with an impression of Africa when I left, it would overwhelmingly be because of people like him.

My dad returned a confused expression, which the man noticed and responded to immediately. Holding out his hand as a subtle reassurance, he stopped laughing long enough to explain. "Sorry, but when you see him, you will understand

9

why I am laughing about it. Come, come this way and you can meet him and see if you would like to take him."

"OK," dad said, which was the signal to proceed. The man walked up to the metal gate, which was large and oblong and appeared more like a cattle gate. He lifted some rope and swung it open for us to pass.

"My name is Joshua, I work with your father at the factory," he said to my mother and I, before walking on, but always still smiling. I guessed his life was good and he knew it, and was content in what he had. It was a rare thing for anyone, from any country, and a good way to be, I thought.

Again we travelled up a mud path, but this time a little narrower, and shadowed either side by huge trees. At the end we could see a small brick house, plain and square, with a few smaller wooden ones around. There was a goat tied to a post by a piece of thin rope, chewing what was left of the wiry grass. It seemed very thin, but happy enough. A large woman walked past, but didn't look at us. I have no idea who she was and Joshua never said anything. I had expected my dad to give him my name, and my mother's, but he never did. As pleasant as they were, Joshua and dad together, he behaved in a certain way, an invisible barrier between us which neither one crossed.

Joshua stopped and looked at us, holding his arms out, ready to talk to us as if we were schoolchildren, and he was the headmaster.

"Now, the dog belonged to my father, and he had him for a long time. He has his ways, and is very quiet, very loving with children. Sadly we have no space for him to be here," he explained, before turning to a small open front brick shed.

Dad didn't say a word, but I had the impression that he knew what to expect. Joshua went into the shed, and after a moment brought out the dog I had been waiting so long for. He was a kind of worn black, I say worn because it was actually tints of grey all round his coat. He wasn't a young dog, and we wouldn't be going on any long runs together, that was for sure. He had this look about him, his expression and his eyes, which suggested he had seen it all, but also that he was a nice affable dog.

Joshua had him tied to a piece of rope, which seemed to be the in thing here, goats on rope, gates on rope, dogs on rope. I wondered if he had children on rope too, but didn't say so, I knew my dad wouldn't appreciate it.

"What's his name?" I asked, because naturally it's the first thing you think of, or at least it's the first thing I do.

"He doesn't actually have a proper name, my father just called him dog."

"Doesn't your dad want him any more?" I asked, which being the age I was wasn't the kind of thing one should do because I might not like the answer. Too late though, I had done it.

"I well, my father died two weeks ago, which is why I have him here. He has nowhere else to go," Joshua explained, and throughout he remained cheerful and positive, understanding my age and ignoring my lack of sensitivity.

"Sorry," mum said, though at the time I still had no idea what she was apologising for.

"No, it's fine. We buried him around the back there, so he's still with us."

I was a little slower to pick things up back then, and genuinely thought he was referring to the dog, but felt confused how he would be stood there on a rope if he was buried around the back. I got there in the end.

"He's a friendly, loving dog, but he needs a new home," Joshua explained, looking at us expectantly.

I could see from the expression on my father's face that he wasn't too impressed. Being old and probably a bit slow, perhaps stuck in his ways, we would have to adapt to him, not he to us.

"I like him," I said, before anyone else could say anything. I knew if I hadn't said that, my dad would very likely have made a polite excuse and left, and the chances were I would never have gotten a dog. I just looked at him, trying to give the impression I saw it as a done deal.

In the end he agreed, however reluctant and took hold of the rope. I didn't hear anything else they discussed, all I could think about was our new dog, called *dog*. I determined that would have to change.

Joshua saw us back to our car, watched dog climb into the back with me, sitting there as if he were only in need of a seat belt to travel in style. Cars back then didn't have back seat belts, so he would have to make do. Mum and dad got into the car, waved off Joshua and drove away.

Back we went up the winding, bumpy road full of holes, and that in itself was an experience. Because the road was so bad, dog kept sliding all around on the seat, and I was sat next to him. He was something like a Labrador, but very large, as if he had spent his life doing nothing but eating, and piled it all on. As we went through over each large bump or through a low dip, the dog would slide into the door, or back over to me, still sat up like a colossus, sliding this way and that, crashing into me. I kept giggling each time be barrelled into me, and then slid away again like some cartoon character. What made it all the funnier was how he just sat there, looking ahead out of the front window, not a care in the world, like a ship rolling in the sea, oblivious to crashing into the rocks that was myself. By the time we got to the top of the road I was unable to stop laughing, it was so silly. I half expected dog to burst out laughing, but of course he didn't, it was all quite serious to him.

I guess to him, it was just another step in a long and eventful life. For me it was a sign of things to come.

CHAPTER TWO

By the time we got back to the house, two things were apparent. Firstly, that we should have taken drinks with us, because we were all parched, including the dog, and secondly, that he was a very muddy, very dusty dog, and really needed a wash. I had visions of us putting him into the bath and giving him a good scrub, but that wasn't in dad's plans, he figured hosepipe and a bit of soap.

We all wandered into the house, dog in tow, me holding his rope. As soon as we got into the house it was immediately much cooler and welcome for it. The houses are built with red brick tiles, and everything else was white to reflect the heat. Once into the hallway, the kitchen area was to the right, the bedrooms and bathroom to the left down a longer hall. Ahead to the right was a small dining room, and down a few steps ahead and left was the large living room, with a huge open brick fire, which would never get used.

I walked down the steps to the living room, bringing dog with me. I sat on the large yellow sofa, and unfastened his rope. Many dogs with collars have a mark on their fur after a few years, where it wears in. This dog didn't have anything like that, so I figured he had roamed freely.

"Don't let him on the sofa," dad ordered, before retreating into the kitchen to get a drink. The moment he left, dog climbed straight away onto the sofa, turned around quickly and dropped like a sack of spuds onto it, laying right across as if it were his own personal bed. I jumped up, grabbed a hold of him as best I could and tried to pull him off, but he was having none of it. He just looked at me, bleary eyed, as if I were a mere fly that needed ignoring. He was comfy and nothing was going to change that.

My mum and dad both walked out of the kitchen, to the hall at the top of the living room stairs, drinking Sprite from a bottle. Immediately their eyes caught sight of the great dusty black and grey beast revelling in his new home and me stood there like a lemon not knowing quite what to do or say.

"Down, get down off there," dad shouted, but the dog didn't care, he just laid there, taking up all the room.

Eventually my dad had to go down to him, stand right in front of him, shout at him three times and push him as hard as he could before he finally flopped off onto the floor. It wasn't just that he was old, or that he was tired, it was just this dog's way. He would only do things as and when he wanted. If I hadn't seen him with my own eyes, I would have been sure he was a cat, he was so wayward.

Mum went to the back door, which was actually all black metal, and opened up the double doors, allowing a flood of heat to rush in. Out back were some white wooden chairs with padded cushions on them and a big round white wooden table. In one corner was a long green hosepipe, permanently connected to fixed brass cold water tap. Either side of our garden and all the way down was a huge dark brown wooden fence, around fifteen feet high. Dad took ages trying to coax dog into the garden, but eventually with the aid of some treats-pieces of meat cut from the meal we would have later, he succeeded. Dog made his way to the small bone on offer on the ground, but before he could enjoy it, my dad unleashed the freezing cold water over him, soaking him head to toe. Dog must have been used to such things, because he barely flinched, simply standing there, as a waterfall drenched over him. I was then handed the bar of soap and told to get to work. I did so, reluctantly, rubbing it into his thick, heavy coat, lathering him up in a way I didn't think he had ever had before. Dog just stood, tongue out, panting away. He had this weird fixed expression, like a thousand yard stare, where it didn't matter if the world was ending or whether there was a meal the size of a car, whichever way he would just look at you in the same weary way, as if he just was too tired or disinterested to show how he really felt.

It didn't matter though, because as my dad washed the soap off and his coat began to shine, all I could think was, we have our own dog, and I was going to learn to love him very quickly.

Once the water was turned off, dog instinctively wandered off to the grass, into the hot sun. It was afternoon by then, and extremely hot in the naked sunshine. Dog flopped down again and laid on his side, barely even able to break out into any kind of movement. Most dogs would squirm around on their backs, shifting this way and that, but he was far too big and lumbering for that, and just a little bit lazy.

That was the wonderful thing about Africa, most of the time it stayed warm, and when the sun was out it was so hot you didn't need towels to dry. Of course when the rainy season came it was cold, cloudy and miserable, but even then I was impressed by the ferocity of its intensity.

I sat in the big white garden chair, on a huge padded blue cushion and watched him, wondering what might happen if I should throw a ball. Disappointingly, not much I expected.

"Come on, we're off out to the shops," my mum called. She had really gotten into the Africa thing, well at least the tourist Africa thing. We had only been there a very short time and she had covered the living room with matt black ornaments made by locals, showing people fishing or just sitting weaving or something. They did look like the kind of thing people from abroad might buy, but they were still nice. Mum typically wore cotton dresses and sandals because they were cool against the hot air, but the Africa continent patterns were just like a lot of things, which said a lot of nothing about the country we had chosen to live in. No matter really, at least she was happy. In differing ways we all were.

"What about Dog?" I asked. As soon as I said his odd name out loud, Dog, it struck me how bad it was. "Can we change his name?" I asked. Mum looked at me confused, not knowing which to answer first, if at all.

"Come on, he'll be fine," she said disappearing inside. I followed her in, looked back at him laid there like a giant flat furry suitcase, not a care in the world, and felt my first twinge of affection for him. We had only just got him, but he was already growing on me. He was like some cartoon character.

We went and got into the car and drove out of the gates. The front of the place had these large black iron gates. I have no idea what they were supposed to represent, but I guess they thought it was safer, whoever owned the house. The small tarmac area outside the front of our house went straight up, steeply, then onto a long road leading both ways. To the right went to the bottom of the estate and from that to the wilderness beyond. To the left wound around what had become a huge estate, and towards town, but also a route out of Nairobi, and if you travelled far enough, right across Kenya and to the coastal city of Mombasa.

We headed steadily towards town, but all I could think of was Dog; what to call him, and whether he would be alright there by himself. The house was well fenced in, so he couldn't simply run away, but I wondered still. I couldn't help it.

As we drove along the roads, very often there would be empty fields beside, and it seemed on every corner there was something growing, usually banana plants. We never stopped long enough to see if there were fruit on them, but I suspected there was, there were so many of them. As we drove we passed people walking along the side of the roads. Back then it was common to see white people or Asians driving, but you would rarely see any Africans driving, unless they were Police or politicians. Those who did walk alongside the road were mostly barefoot, but it was very common for them to be dressed in highly colourful clothes. Being close to such a built up and reasonably settled area like Nairobi, I never saw any locally there in what I had expected, traditional tribal clothes, or anything similar to what I had seen in films. They just seemed like me, other than so many of them not having shoes. I would later learn more about that.

As we drove to a crossroads, there were some young boys playing, about four of them, and I could see them picking up stones to throw towards the banana plants. It seemed like they were having fun, in a way I wouldn't have minded joining in with.

My dad slowed the car as we approached. I thought initially it was because he was going to watch out for oncoming traffic. Instead, he actually stopped driving altogether. He wound down the window and just looked at these boys. I had no idea what was going on, and I don't think my mum did either, but we rarely ever argued with dad, he tended to not take it well.

After a minute, I slid over in the back seat to try see what was going on. I could see a small dog, running around, this way and that, as these boys threw small sticks and pebbles at it. I wasn't sure if they were playing with it, or the dog thought they were, or if they were being horrible towards it. Either way it looked wrong.

"Hey, stop that," my dad shouted. He remained sat in the car, arm leaning out of the open window. Being in a new country, not knowing what might happen, you would think that he would show a degree of caution, for how people might react, but he never did, always jumping in feet first and thinking later.

The boys looked at him, I think a little surprised at his intervention. They just looked but didn't say anything. I had no idea if they spoke English, but it was very common in Kenya that most people did, as well as Swahili, which said a lot about them as a country, their abilities and their open nature. We loved it.

At least they had stopped throwing stones at the dog. My dad, being unpredictable, opened the car door and stood out. I think in England if someone had done that we would have run away, but these boys, they just seemed a little shocked, and of course curious about what he was up to. They just continued to stand there watching him.

"Don't throw stones at him, it's not nice," dad continued, like a schoolteacher scolding his class. I didn't really react, I had no idea what to do, it was all so new to me. He looked at them, as they looked at him, nobody reacting, and being the impatient type, did what he often does, and that was act without thinking. He walked over to this small dog, bent over, picked it up, came back to the car, opened the back door, and threw it in, onto my lap. I nearly jumped out of my skin over it. Wow.

I didn't touch the dog as it paced around on the back seat, padding over me like I was a piece of furniture. Dad casually got back into the car, closed the door and drove off. He didn't even look back, just drove as if we had stopped by for a bag of fruit.

What can I say? I was a teenager, and had never argued with my dad before, so I wasn't used to voicing an opinion on things like this, so I just sat there, in awe of it all, wanting to say things but not daring. My mum was a bit like me, she didn't often contradict Dad, but I could imagine she was also a bit shocked.

After we drove for a few minutes, I couldn't help it, I had to say something. "What are we going to do with it?"

My dad just carried on driving, none of us saying another word. The little dog was black too, like the big one we had picked up. I just couldn't believe my eyes, here was I so excited in the morning to have got a dog, and here we were by the morning another dog sat in the car beside me. It was crazy.

"What if the people he belongs to want him back?" I asked, which was a fair question.

"Well then they shouldn't throw stones at him," was all he said. Rightly or wrongly, he had seen a dog being abused, and made his mind up over it, and that was that.

We drove to town still, and I waited in the car with the dog while they got stuff. They weren't gone long, but I never did a thing, I was too afraid to even speak to it. Looking back, obviously it might be considered foolish to take in a stray dog in this way, what with all the possibility of diseases, but also without knowing how their temperament might be, how they might react. I guess on that day it didn't matter, and long term looking back we got lucky.

I was sat there, windows down enough that I could cope with the heat, but not so low that he might jump out and run off. He seemed as excited as I was, and for a dog was unlike anything I could ever remember seeing. He didn't altogether look like a dog, he was a very unusual cross, with very odd features. He was about the size of a large terrier, but was thin with it, and a flat black matted coat like a Staffordshire bull Terrier. That was the only similarity though, because he had a long thin tail which ended at a point and always seemed to point in the opposite direction his head was pointing. He had thin legs, and the strangest looking head I had ever seen. He had tiny black ears, and long pointed head, more like a large mouse head than a dog. Altogether he was very unusual, but I liked how energetic and spritely he was, bouncing all over the car, looking out of one window and then to the next. It was like he had begun an adventure, and knew it very well.

Mum and Dad returned with some bags of things, as well as two trays of bottles of soft drinks. Dad opened the boot of the car, which was actually a tailgate, lifting up so that I could see inside. In one of the bags were large chunks of what seemed to be bones, some with meat on them.

"Are they for us?" I asked, because that's what I was like back then, full of the daftest questions. OK, I'm still full of daft questions, but over the years I learned to keep them to myself.

"Yes, we're going to have old bones with little meat on them for dinner," my dad said, slamming the boot closed. It dawned on me that they were for the dogs, and then it finally sunk in that we really were keeping these dogs. I could barely catch my breath, that in one day we were bringing home two dogs. Things in life had such a habit back then of changing so rapidly it seemed like a dream. Little did I know how much of an adventure was about to begin.

CHAPTER THREE

Before I even had time to celebrate the arrival of our odd shaped twins, my dad dropped the packs of bottles onto the kitchen counter and turned to me. "By the way, you're going to school soon," he said, before carrying on unpacking. As surprises go, it was hardly the biggest, but there went my dreams of a life of ease and freedom. It didn't matter where you went in the world, even to the supposed wilds of Africa, you could never escape the simple choice of either school or work.

I looked at Mum, with those pleading eyes, which always worked on her, but never on him. "We're going out this weekend to check a few schools, to see if there is one to suit," she said, and I knew then there was nothing to change it.

It was late on the Friday, going into the weekend. That would be my last time of freedom, as I saw it, but at least now I had something new to deal with.

When we had got out of the car neither of my parents seemed the least bit bothered about this new dog in the back with me. It seemed unreal, I could barely contain my excitement over it, but looking back on it now I can see how daft it was in a way, because there was no telling what diseases the dog might have had or its temperament. Anything could have happened, and it did, but thankfully only in a good way.

This tiny dog was an unusual mix, it behaved more like a cat, showing affection when he wanted to and ignoring you if you wanted to play. On that first day all he wanted to do was wander around the front gardens and sniff at things. It seemed dogs heaven, sniffing at all sorts of things. I could only imagine what kind of smells it would discover in a place like Africa.

I went through the house and opened up the back doors to see the other dog laid out there, acting as if we had never been gone, sleeping away, clearly enjoying the heat. I went back to the kitchen, got a large bucket of water for him, before realizing I would have to get something that suited them both. I shuffled around in the cupboards before pulling out a wide flat bowl and filled it with water. Slowly I took it out and put it down onto the paving at the back. The small dog came trotting around the side to the back, free as a breeze, not a care in the world, looking as if he had just discovered his ability to enjoy open spaces. The larger dog just laid still, lifting his head a fraction, I think to see if the bowl contained food. As it didn't he flopped back down again, closed his eyes and resumed his sloppy snoring.

The small dog paced right up to the bowl, sniffed a moment, before lapping at it. It was big enough for them both, with plenty of fresh clean water, but undeterred he drank, and drank, and drank, until it was almost gone. I burst out laughing, not believing a small dog like that could take in so much water. I pictured his belly hanging down on the floor if he took much more in, dragging along as he tried to trot away.

Mum and Dad had finished putting things away and made their way out to join us. They were stood at the doorway watching the small dog drink and the large one lying there like an old carpet waiting for someone to wipe their feet on him.

"We'll have to think of names for them," my dad said. It was only at that point that it sank in that they were ours, to keep, that come what may, we had enlarged our family. I could really begin to feel something proper for them.

"This small one will also need a bath," Mum said, which sounded like a good idea, because he was pretty smelly and being in Kenya dogs were prone to fleas and things.

"I'll do it," I said quickly, wanting to give him a good scrub so I could give them a hug afterwards.

"Right, I'll get some shampoo," my mum said, but before she could leave my dad interrupted her.

"What can we call them though, can't call them dog one and dog two can we?" he insisted.

I had always been an avid reader of comics, getting them delivered weekly, at the same time as my parents' newspapers. One of the most favourite comic for years had a character in it called Sammy Shrink, who was a little boy who was only six inches tall. The comic was Whizzer and Chips, and I read it for years. For some odd reason it popped into my head to call them Sammy and Shrink, big dog being Sammy and little dog being Shrink.

"How about Sammy and Shrink?" I asked, not entirely seriously. Both of my parents knew who these characters were, because I had read them so long and those comics had been instrumental in my learning how to read. I loved them so much I ended up learning to read so that I could understand what was going on. I didn't expect them to taken any notice of it, and imagined we would be calling them Rex or Lassie or something equally normal for dogs.

"That's a good idea," my mother said immediately, to my complete surprise.

"Yeah, OK, that's what we'll call them," my dad agreed. You can imagine my pleasant surprise that I had been able to choose not one dog's name but two, and as funny as they sounded, that's what they ended up being called.

Little Shrink had stopped lapping up the entire contents of the water bowl long enough to sniff at big Sammy, laid there still as if he were a piece of furniture. At least they weren't fighting, which had been a concern.

As I went to take a hold of Shrink, to lift him up for a hug, my dad stepped in. "Not yet, let's give him a bath," he insisted. Hugs would have to wait.

Mum went indoors to get the shampoo, as Dad followed her. I looked at both dogs and could barely contain my happiness, it was amazing to have the two of them. I headed in, ready to go to the bathroom, to run some hot water and mix in a little cold, so we could give them a good scrub.

Just as I was about to turn down towards the bathroom my dad caught me. "Where are you going? Aren't you coming to wash the dog?" he asked.

"Yeah, I'm about to run the bath, get some hot water in there," I replied. He burst out laughing, quite loudly, as was his way.

"No, don't be daft, we're washing him outside, with a hosepipe, like Sammy."

It didn't sound like such a great plan to me, but when I thought about it, it could be a lot more fun this way.

"OK, I'll go get changed," I said, running off. I had been wearing jeans and a t-shirt, which I was more accustomed to, but being outside in such a hot place, especially with a hosepipe going, shorts were definitely the order of the day. I would often want to go without a top, but the sun was so hot I would end up getting burnt quickly, so it was rarely an option even with suntan lotion.

By the time I got outside again Shrink was sat on the grass, I guess looking at his surroundings, and Sammy had finally risen to just look at us, probably wondering why we were working so hard when it was so hot. I think to him work was actually doing something, anything at all, because walking was very difficult thing to do.

Dad had picked up the hosepipe. As hot as it was outside, the water was still pretty cold.

"Should I get a bowl with some warm water in it, to mix for him?" I asked. His being so small made me think he wouldn't appreciate it as much as Sammy did.

"No, he will be fine," he insisted. He wasn't one who would listen to anyone who didn't agree with them, and just turned on the tap, sending out a stream of cold water all over. Immediately Sammy knew what was coming and upped and went. I've never seen him move so fast, before or after. I guess one bath was enough for him.

Neither dog had any kind of collar. I remember wondering at the time if it meant he had never properly belonged to anyone, and that was why he sometimes would appear distant in nature. Both dogs had that about them, which was different to the attentiveness I had witnessed from dogs as pets at home with others.

"Get a hold of Shrink and bring him over," my father suggested. I ran over and grabbed hold of him, at first with one hand, and pulled, but he just stood there, looking away in the opposite direction, thinking *nope, not doing that.* I then took hold of him with both hands, and pulled, tugging on his as much as I could.

"Come on, don't mess around," Dad said. I think he thought I was doing it on purpose, but I wasn't. It was like trying to tame a mini dinosaur. I pulled and pulled, but Shrink just stood there. I really think he had no idea how hard it was to deal with him, especially as I was so thin I looked like a collection of pipes in clothes.

In the end I went round the back of him, placed two hands on his bottom and shoved. I leaned down, pushed into him, and shoved suddenly to make him move quickly before he could disagree. He wasn't as daft as he looked, because just as I went to shove, he craned his neck around, looked at me, figured how daft I was and shifted sideways. I fell to the floor like a sack of flour with a big thud. Sammy and my father just stood there looking at me, I think wondering which of us was the idiot.

I picked myself up off the muddy coarse grass and dusted myself down. Before I could go in for round two my mother appeared at the door. She had two small bones, one in each hand. "Here, come get it," she said simply and the stampeded began. Thinking Sammy couldn't move that fast proved very wrong, as he leapt like a horse towards her, sitting on his best behaviour right in front of her. Shrink, as always loved his food, but he would never betray his cat tendencies, so slowly walked over, at his ease, and stood looking, fully expecting everything that was coming to him. I think even if he didn't get fed he wouldn't have shown much reaction, he would just had gone off and sat again watching the world go by.

Sammy actually sat and made a big effort to give a paw, without even being asked, so he showed he had been looked after by someone, even if not as a pet. My mother leaned over and went to give him the bone, and he took it so gently you would think it was a Prince kissing the hand of a Princess.

As promised my mother gave him the bone. He was such a gentle character that he took it slowly and laid down onto the ground, ignoring everything and everyone as he munched on it. It never occurred to me to wonder whether anyone had ever given him a bath. Life wasn't always easy for a dog in Africa, not all of them were kept as pets, or loved in the way we would grow to.

Eventually both dogs settled and I think really enjoyed their respective shower/ baths. They got all soapy, possibly for the first time, and all that rubbing in and lathering I think both really loved it. Shrink even stopped chewing on what was left of his bone and looked up, eyes struggling to stay open, tale even managing to wag as I washed. He looked like the regal prince of dogs enjoying a royal wash from his subjects. I half expected a roar that never came.

Finally my father washed all the soap off him, and stood back. Sammy finished the last morsel of his bone and while still chewing lumbered up and walked away, before giving an almighty shake. Then he did something I would never have expected of him, this great sofa of a dog actually broke into a run and crashed to the ground on the grass, spinning over onto his back, rubbing himself madly for fun.

Shrink followed suit, jumping onto the grass before flopping to the ground, legs flopping all over in the air, as the unending sun made steam ride from his fur. I just laughed, because I hadn't expected it. The more I saw of him the more I loved him.

The moment all of us turned to look at him, his little pointy ears shot up, as if he had heard something unusual. This was one of those times when he wasn't daft, at least not when it counted. Up went his little bottom, ready and walking away, nice and easy as if he were just going for a quick walk and would be back in time for tea.

"Shrink, got a bone for you," my mother shouted, but he was having none of it. The bones was tiny compared to Sammy, but it looked as big as one of Shrink's legs. He would likely dine on it for days on end, but he didn't care.

I chased after him, laughing, intent on picking him up, but as soon as he saw me coming for him he sprinted away. I expected he would have been chased more than once in his life, especially after what we saw of the young boys throwing things at him. Besides those I could only imagine what might have tried to get him in Africa, being so small and weedy, he would never have been able to fight for himself. So instead he had learned how to evade capture, and I learned just how good he was at it.

The back garden was open at the side so you could walk around it to the large front area. Most of it was tarmacked, with rock walls around it and plants inside. Steps cut through in between these, and outside of it at the front were the large iron gates which were always closed, and fences surrounding all of this, a good five metres high. So no matter where he ran, he couldn't escape. The fences were there for our protection, but also to keep wild animals out, whatever they may be.

Shrink was like a mountain goat. The moment he saw me coming he burst into a short sprint, and once away from me sufficiently he slowed again, glanced cheekily back and carried on moving. He certainly was never one to do more than he had to. The moment I got close enough to him to make a grab, he hopped onto the one of the rockery areas, crept quickly along and dropped onto the tarmac. I could barely get onto the rockery fast enough, let alone over them and close in on him.

My dad, not being known for his patience had called out to me while I was playing silly fools, but I had been having so much fun chasing Shrink I hadn't had time to respond. He had dropped the hosepipe and walked around to see where we had got to. I think in his eyes I was sat there cuddling little doggy and getting to know my new pal, but of course in real life I had been chasing after Shrink like a runaway chicken.

"Pick him up," my father shouted, walking quickly, as if he would just dive in there and show me how it was done.

I jumped onto the rockery then down to the tarmac as Shrink trotted off towards the main gates, feeling light as a daisy and as happy as a bee. I ran towards him, as he circled around, still giving me that knowing glance, and circling around the outside of the drive. Dad went the opposite way, giving me a look that suggested I was hopeless and should step back as he did his thing, so I did.

Shrink paused for a moment, and I really thought he had accepted the game was up as my dad leaned over, quickened his pace and went to grab him. Just as I was about to feel all sheepish and congratulate him, Shrink burst ahead, right through his legs and away. Dad grabbed at thin air, before trying to grab underneath himself. It was a sight, as if he were a huge balloon figure deflating at his failure. I giggled for a second, an outburst I hadn't meant, but the glaring look I got suggested he wasn't amused. As he turned to go after Shrink, who by now had once again disappeared back round the side of the house, I followed my father, smiling to myself. Funny, because I knew who was boss then.

As we both went quickly around to the back of the house, to see where Shrink had gotten to finally, we were struck by what we saw. There was Shrink, huge bone in his mouth, sat there, good as gold.

Again I laughed, as he struggled to nibble on such a large bone. It seemed he didn't dare drop it in case Sammy pinched it. Sammy had eaten his bone, and was laid, with a look about him that suggested he was indeed ready to pinch Shrink's bone, and eat him up too.

We walked over to see, as my dad shrugged. He turned to me and looked at me. "See, you could have done that," he said, before walking away as if he hadn't done anything. I just looked at my mother, and she returned the look. She knew what he was like, and we just smiled.

What a day. I couldn't wait to see what came next.

CHAPTER FOUR

In my wildest dreams I couldn't have imagined what did happen. I went indoors, tired from all the heat, and flopped down on the sofa, falling fast asleep. While I was in dreamland, mum and dad went out again, having kindly locked me in. I woke to hear their return, clattering and banging around. They had carrier bags of stuff.

"Where did you go?" I asked, as usual being ignored. They had more important things to do, such as empty the car.

27

"We went to check out some schools," Dad said eventually. "We found one, you start Monday."

My heart leapt. I was both horrified and intrigued at once, wondering about new friends, but dreading the thought of study. I imagine being taught in Swahili by African teachers, angry at me because I hadn't learnt their language already. I was foolish of course, because nearly everyone seemed to speak English, and they all did at that school.

"It's called Saint Mary's Catholic Boys School," my dad said, gulping down a mouth full of Seven-Up from a bottle.

I looked at him, confused. "Am I Catholic then?" I asked in all honesty. Both my parents laughed.

"No, but you don't have to be to go there, they take all faiths," my mum explained. I was none the wiser, but any school wasn't going to be great, because at that age who would want more school, especially on a permanent holiday like I was on.

"What about the dogs?" I asked.

"No, they don't take dogs," mum chipped in quick as a flash. My dad laughed but I didn't find it funny.

"No I mean what will they do during the day when I'm not there."

"Sunbathe no doubt," My dad said, continuing with the theme of mocking me.

"They will be here with me," mum said. I thought about asking some more, but decided not to given how it had gone so far.

I shrugged my shoulders and went to walk away.

"Before you go, they have a uniform. You need to try it on," mum explained. My heart sank. I had worn what seemed like a uniform at my old school, dark blazer, grey trousers, white shirt and a tie I never wore.

"Right," I said in resignation. She picked up a white plastic bag and handed it to me.

"There are some black shoes for you too, I think they're the right size."

I took the bag, feeling pretty flat and went to try them on. It was a dark day indeed. When I got them on I came straight back, to see my dad sat at the dining room table and mum sat on the sofa with both dogs at her feet. They both looked straight at me as I stood at the top of the steps.

"Oh, that's nice, you look really smart," Mum said. Dad didn't say a word. He didn't need to. My uniform consisted of a baggy khaki coloured shirt with huge pockets on the front. The socks were thick woollen green things, and worst of all, I had to wear shorts, long ones that just stopped over my knees. Also khaki. I wasn't sure if they were meant to stop at the knees, or be higher up or lower, but whichever they looked spectacularly awful. I felt like I was supposed to have the appearance of an intrepid African explorer, but in actual fact looked like a silly character out of a cartoon.

"Can't I have trousers?" I asked, hoping without much hope.

"Apparently it's their policy. All the pupils have this kind of thing," my dad said. If he thought it was as bad as I did, he kept it to himself.

"What about the teachers, do they wear these?" I asked trying not to look at myself.

"Oh no," mum said happily. "They're priests, they wear long dresses," she explained, smiling.

"Cassocks," my dad said quickly.

"No need to swear," mum said. I had no idea if she meant it or was joking, but either way I was lost. I wasn't sure about being away from my new dogs, let alone having to wear this uniform. It would keep me cool but it wouldn't *look* cool.

So that was the start of one thing and the end of another. I had a weekend to get as much fun in with the dogs as I could. I was determined to make the most of it.

I went back to my bedroom, got changed into my jeans and t-shirt and deliberately dropped the uniform on the floor. It stayed there until I was forced to wear it again for the start of school.

I ran back into the living room, to find mum had gone into the kitchen to cook some tea for us. My dad had gone for a lie down, so I was alone with the dogs. Shrink was laid near the large open fireplace. He had his little front paws out, laying on them, and his back legs sticking right out. I thought it funny how streamlined he looked, but his eyes were tightly closed and he seemed very much at peace.

Sammy seemed not to like hard floors. He kept pacing around, unable to settle. The fur on his elbows were worn away, so I figured he must be used to sleeping on hard surfaces. Wouldn't mean he liked it though I guess.

I went to the back door to open it up as it was stifling hot inside. I turned back, just in time to see Sammy lifting his front paw onto the sofa. My first thought was to say something quickly to him to get down, because I knew he wasn't allowed up. No dogs or pets on the furniture, that seemed to be the unwritten rule.

Before I could react he had his other paw on the sofa, and was somehow shuffling himself forward to climb fully onto it. I was struck by his snail like pace, as he struggled to pull himself up. Once he had gotten so far on, he tried lifting his back leg up, but couldn't connect it high enough to get onto the top cushion, and dropped back again. Next up he tried lifting his other leg, lifting it as high as he could get it, realizing it was too high and he couldn't do it, so gave up. So there he was, stood there two legs on the sofa, his body half on it, and two legs stood on the rug in front of the sofa. I just burst out laughing, trying not to be so loud that I would attract attention.

He looked at me, which I think was the first time he had actually done that, made proper eye contact. I think he wanted me to go round and give him a little shove up, push that big bottom onto the comfy seat so he could feel the luxury of it. I didn't fancy getting any hassle over him being there, and being partly responsible, so instead just watched to see what he would do. It seemed to have been too much for him, that mighty exertion, so he opened his mouth, flopped out his tongue and began panting as if he had run a mile.

Sammy then tried laying his head down on the seat, but it was too much of a struggle. Once again the back leg gave a little shuffle up and down, but just as he was possibly about to succeed, a large sound interrupted us both in our delights.

"No, get down," came the sound. It was my dad, not the least bit pleased, and looking the worse for wear for his ill advised nap. The heat often drained our energy, and during our time there we would often need to have a sleep, but the trouble with that is when you wake up you tended to feel worse than when you went to sleep.

Big Sammy just looked at him as if he were talking to someone else, that he didn't have any rules to abide by other than the ones he liked. My dad walked down the few steps to the living room and approached him. "Down," he barked, making me think he was deliberately lightening the mood over it. I was wrong.

My dad put his hand around him and pulled him off abruptly. Sammy was so soft he wouldn't hurt a fly, just looking like a great log being rolled away down a slip. To him it was all good, he could adapt to anything. It was one of the things I most liked about him, that come what may, whatever Africa could throw at him, he would always come through it and just be the plain happy go lucky dog he always was. I admired him, even though he was only a dog.

My dad wasn't overly harsh, but he could be strict when he wanted, and right then he took Sammy and pushed him out of the back door, closing it. Sammy stood there looking in with an expression that was impossible to read. I don't think he was impressed, but once again we were back with the doors closed in the stifling heat. You might imagine a place like that would have ceiling fans or something, but nope, nothing, we never did.

I felt sorry for Sammy, but had no time to think much about it before my dad carried on.

"Don't let him on the furniture," he insisted, walking away before I could deny being a part of it. I thought about asking if Shrink could go on there, as being a teenager I was waking up to the idea that adults weren't always right, and that I had a right to a say in things too. I didn't say anything, I didn't want to make it worse for the dogs. I was just so happy to have them, no need to spoil that.

Shrink had woken up to the noise and was stretching and yawning. He was funny when he yawned, because his little mouth was so pointed it made him look like some strange mythical creature, not at all like a dog. I have no idea if he had been aware of the noise from my dad, but it brought about a very different reaction. I thought he was going to hide, but instead he sidled up to me rubbing against me. It was such a surprise, and so cute, I hadn't thought he would ever do it, because he never seemed to show us much attention. Obviously he had only just arrived, but from the moment we got him he seemed to be in his own little world, that I never expected much affection from him. It was also a show of intelligence, that he could see there was an issue, I was the focus of it, and he kind of lent support. I loved that.

"I didn't let him," I said, which was the first time we had disagreed about anything, or at least the first time I had felt the courage to answer him back. It was a kind of crossing point, where I knew in myself I had the right to speak up, and for the first time could stand my ground for what I thought was right and wrong. He ignored me and walked off, but I knew it mattered, and he had heard me.

I opened the back door, to see Sammy stood there. I suspect if I hadn't opened the door he may well have stood there for hours looking in. He was a funny sort of dog, that as big and quite old as he was he would easily stand and do nothing for ages. He could sleep with the best of them, but if he had to stand around he would do, no matter how long.

I smiled at him and he looked at me, though I couldn't say if the look was asking to come in, or for food, or whether his mind was actually blank and he was staring into space. With that dog, you never knew.

I walked into the garden and sat on one of the patio chairs, as Shrink followed me. Again he sat near me, though this time not leaning against me. I guess he had made his point. Sammy allowed himself the luxury of turning, like an oil tanker taking hours to do so, he took his own good time over it to look at me. So I was sat, with these two dogs looking at me, and I have no idea what they expected, a show maybe, and I just couldn't stop myself laughing at them. It was amazing to have them, because it still hadn't sunk in just what we had done, where we were, and now much our lives had changed. It felt like I had friends to share things with, someone I could talk to and they would listen. Not that I gave them much choice!

I got up to go get some things, but before I could get in Sammy showed an uncharacteristic turn of speed and rushed back into the house. He was like a house on legs trotting in, back to the sofa. There must have been something very attractive about that sofa to him, because he never did leave it alone. He just stood there, in front of it, looking at me, waiting for permission. I had half a mind to tell him to jump on, but didn't because it just wasn't worth the hassle.

I went into the kitchen where mum was sorting things and got some snacks and a drink, and went to go back to the garden.

"We'll be having tea soon," she said. I liked the idea of it, as I was feeling very hungry.

"What are we having?" I asked, imagining all the food that I would any moment be eating.

"We have potatoes, and beef, but we forgot to get some vegetables," mum replied. I wasn't too bothered by the lack of veg, I rarely enjoyed anything like it from a tin or which had been frozen.

"We can go cut some from the garden," my dad said, walking into the kitchen. It was small and immediately felt overcrowded. After his reaction to Sammy being on the sofa I wasn't too keen on speaking, but I certainly was alerted to that idea.

"We can't go into that garden, it's not safe," mum said. She was no doubt right in some respects, but common sense never stopped my dad. Ever.

"Nah, it'll be fine, come on, let's go and have a look at what there is."

The main back garden outside the house was quite proper, with a white picket fence at the end, but beyond the small gate was a huge narrow field, with a steep bank of grass running down it, and stone steps. Once at the bottom it was fairly flat, with things growing nearest and then the stream dividing it, and beyond that quite a large expanse of corn.

My dad led the way down the steps, advising us to be careful just as he tripped and nearly fell himself. I really wanted to laugh, but given how he had been I figured I would just keep the peace. I followed and mum came last, reluctantly.

"Seriously, we don't know what's down there," mum insisted, but it was a kind of adventure. Most pointedly, neither dog followed us, both standing at the top of the steps looking down at us, in more ways than one. I wondered what they might be thinking, but it wouldn't be too hard to figure if they could they would be laughing at us. After all, they knew very well the dangers of Africa and had survived them this far; no small feat for dogs in such a place.

Dad dropped onto the soft soil, as the steps ended and no path had been created. I had on an old pair of trainers with the sole on one foot flipping off, and dad had his work shoes on, not the best of ideas. Mum had kept on her slippers, showing that even she wasn't immune from being foolish.

"These look like sweet potatoes," dad said, stopping to look at rows and rows of greenery. They had been doing so well potatoes were actually sticking out of the ground, fighting to get at the sun. Mum nodded, trying not to fall in the soft ground. She wasn't having the best of times at all.

Before anyone could suggest we go back, dad trotted off again, got to the stream and jumped right over it. It wasn't too big, but it did have steep sides around it and was sunken two feet below. I certainly didn't fancy falling in.

Mum was more of a trooper over it than I was, as she matter-of-factly just waded over there, leapt over the stream and made for where my dad was. If she could I think she would have had her hands on her hips as if to say I told you so and wagged a finger at him. Instead she got there ahead of me and her attention was immediately distracted by all that corn, all of it large and very ripe for picking.

Dad walked over to the high wooden fence and pulled something off it. As he headed back to us I could see it was a machete, with a wooden handle and a very long blade. I had never seen a thing like it before, and had no idea what it did until he showed it to me and explained it. He walked over to a long stem corn plant and leaned over, before hacking away at the base. I have no idea if we were supposed to kill the plant off like that, or just pick the corn from it, but it's what he did, and so we all mucked in. Dad cut the entire stems off, mum dragged them away from where he was hacking, and I was left to pick out the corn. None of us claimed to have any idea what we were doing, but we went for it anyway. The corn was huge, much bigger than those we used to boil in the pan bought from a supermarket. They were tough to pull off, and then were wrapped in tight, strong green leaves.

One by one we went through them all, like a routine. While I was doing that, I was very careful at what I was picking up. I couldn't help but feel how strange it was that we were in a small field in Africa, picking corn, and nobody had mentioned any possible concerns about spiders, snakes or even mosquitoes from the nearby water. We just got on with it, and I guess if anything had happened we would have dealt with it.

"Run back to the house and get a couple of carrier bags for all of this," my dad, and again I nearly laughed. As if I could run in that weather, the sun was so hot it felt like I was going to melt. I did as he asked though, and got some bags, returned and helped fill them.

"There's enough corn here to last us weeks," mum said, but I think dad had wanted to do it not for the food but for the chance to do something African, as he saw it.

We carried it all back, then mum put six pieces of corn on the cob in a large pan and boiled it. I wish I could say it was the best tasting corn ever, but in truth it was just like any other.

When we got back in, Sammy and Shrink followed us eagerly, as if we had been out digging up a giant bone just for them. Corn there being cut fresh didn't smell of anything particularly edible, but I guess both dogs must have had their fair share when cooked, because they didn't move away at all.

"Go lay down," my dad shouted at both dogs as they tried to follow us into the kitchen, but whether they only understood Swahili or just didn't care what he said I don't know, but they certainly ignored him.

As we took the bags into the kitchen, Shrink scrambled deftly in between our feet, this way and that, making sure he was right near the cooker, looking up as if he were watching for any little piece of food dropping, no matter how nasty or small. Clearly he was a survivor, he had been on the streets of Nairobi and its outlier towns and had to fend for himself, which meant not missing a chance of a meal.

Sammy couldn't hope to be as quick and clever, but given he was such a tubby dog, he must have learnt to do something right. He stood outside the kitchen, whether hopeful or daft, I wasn't sure, but he never seemed to panic. The only sign you would get that he was hungry was a long river of drool running from his chops, spilling down onto floor. It was pretty gross, but could I say charming? No.

Mum had primed the beef well, and the potatoes were near cooked, the corn didn't take long and we finally sat and ate. I had been wearing some very odd brown trousers that had a different shade of brown stripe on them. For some reason I was wearing a plain white short sleeved shirt too. By the time we

36

had finished and got in, I was covered in mud. It was dusty dry, but still I was very messy. I had the feeling we were all quite satisfied with ourselves, but to this day I still wonder if he had done the right thing. I also couldn't help but wonder what all those people the opposite side of the huge back fence thought of us, digging up our own food, when most of the other houses on the estate paid people very poor wages to go do it for them. I never did find out.

My dad kindly dropped what was left of one of his cobs to the floor, which Shrink sprang on. There was hardly anything left on it, and as Shrink grabbed it, it seemed like he was trying to pick up a log which was double his size. He was plucky though, never dropping it, dragging it to the wooden floor on the hall where he began to nibble at it.

Mum was a bit kinder, leaning over to hand Sammy a bit of bone from the beef. He gently took it from her, so slowly it seemed as if he were taking a religious artefact from a prophet. He guided it slowly into his mouth, took a hold of it so softly, and walking away. He thanked her with a pile of dribble.

Shrink looked at Sammy eating his bone over by the table and must straight away have realised something was wrong, because all he had got was a gristly piece of corn cob, and Sammy had a nice bone with some meat on it. Shrink jumped straight up and made his way to Sammy, and I thought they were going to have a fight, which I certainly didn't want to see.

Instead Shrink stood over Sammy, watching him like a hawk, occasionally looking back to me as if to say, *what about me?*

Shrink kept circling round Sammy, looking so forlorn and sad by it, he was missing out on such a treat. Just as I thought they would kick off, mum came back from the kitchen with another small bone and handed it to Shrink. No such care and calm here, as Shrink snapped it from her, turned and ran off, before anyone could jump in and steal it. I guess that is what came from being so small, you had to fight for what you got. It was never a sign he was that kind of dog, snappy or ill

37

tempered, just that he wasn't afraid to stand up for his little self. I liked that about him.

Besides those, both dogs got a nice treat with some leftover meat and potatoes, filling them up. Sammy ate his in no time from a large silver metal bowl, then wandered off to sleep it off on the cool hall floor. Shrink managed to finish his bowl, obviously having learned never to leave food, because if you did it would likely be taken by something else. It was a big enough bowl, full of lovely food for him. He struggled to finish it, but managed it in the end, and then when he looked up I just burst out laughing, his stomach was so stuffed that it looked like he was pregnant. He waddled as he walked, his long spindly little legs struggling to keep him going. At first he went to try the steps down to the living room area, but obviously he figured out quickly that wasn't going to work, so turned and ended up going over to where Sammy was laid. Sammy didn't bat an eyelid, he was long gone into the land of nod. Shrink took one look at how nice it was, then flopped down quickly onto the cold floor beside him, and in seconds was well gone, both dogs, snoring like tractors, probably having had the best meals they had ever had. It wouldn't be the last.

I went and got a book and began to read, sat on the sofa. Dad just did some work at the dining room table, and mum sat and tried to watch some TV. Plenty of it was in English, but it was mainly very old seventies programming so not very enjoyable for us.

We just relaxed for the night, and both dogs continued to sleep.

"Right, bed time I think," mum said, as they were both ready, wanting to go.

"I'll just read a bit more," I replied. Mum pulled a face. I was at that age, where my right to choose what I did late in the evening was becoming less a matter for my parents, and more for me to choose. Still, it was a tough one for my mum to come to terms with; I was growing up.

"Leave him, it's fine," my dad said, but mum was having none of it. It wasn't that much of a big deal to me, so I just upped and went to my bedroom. I didn't care enough to argue about it, but in time it would become an issue. That night seemed to be the start of it.

After an hour or so, the entire place was silent. Mum and dad had fallen asleep, struggling to cope with the intense heat, but I was fine with it. I got up to go and get a drink from the kitchen, but when I looked down the steps to the living room, I couldn't believe my eyes at what I saw.

At one end of the sofa was Shrink, all curled up, looking like a little bird tucked safely away in its nest, lightly snoring in complete comfort. What most shocked me, and made me laugh, was Sammy, as he had sprawled out, taking up the entire rest of the sofa, legs poking out, his cheeks pulled back a little exposing his teeth, as if he were really enjoying his time on the soft comfy sofa.

I did find it very funny, but I knew how my dad would react if he saw them, so quickly went down and got hold of Shrink. He was small enough that I could pick him up, and did so. He was lovely and warm there, and really sleepy, like a little baby in my arms. I just picked him up and put him on the rug in front of the sofa, hoping he wouldn't try to get back on. While I was there he didn't anyway.

Sammy was an altogether different proposition. He was such a huge lump, which you wouldn't expect for a Labrador type, and whatever he was crossed with, perhaps a cow, but it left its mark on him, because he was so relaxed all the time, and as heavy as a wrecking ball.

"Sammy, get down," I insisted, not too loud that I might wake someone, but loud enough and with enough of a rasp in my voice that he would understand how important it was and that I really meant. He didn't even open his eyes!

I leaned over him, looking a little closer, staring at him. "Sammy, get... down," I said as loud as I dare, pointing my finger from him to the floor. This time he did open his eyes, and looked at me as if to ask was it time for food.

My next plan of action was to click my fingers. I did so, clicked once loudly, then rasped again to get down. I finished it off with a *now*, big emphasis on the *now*. He opened his eyes, looked up a little, success, he lifted his head, yawned so much his breath filled the air with stale cheese taste. Then he dropped his head back to the sofa and blinked a few times. I think at most he thought I was just annoying.

By then I had been unable to stop myself giggling. He was such a funny dog, like no other I had ever known. I think if he had a liking for music it would have been jazz, totally unpredictable and cool with it. You could throw a ball at him and it would bounce off his head, and he would just look at you as if to ask why you did that?

The last thing I wanted was for him to get into trouble and get shouted at. I could imagine him being kicked out into the garden for the night. It could get very cold at night in Kenya, even during hot periods, and besides there was nothing for him to sleep on.

There was no other choice but to take things into my own hands, literally. I went round the front of him and placed both hands right underneath him. I made a huge effort to lift him off, but he was such a dead weight. He didn't get the message, just laying there like a floppy sack of potatoes, slipping around my hands making it impossible to move him. Besides he was so heavy I doubt my dad could have lifted him.

Plan A had failed, I then placed both hands right round his back and began to pull. I'm not sure if he was doing something to stop me, but I couldn't budge him, it seemed like he had been glued in place. Plan B was a no go.

I then climbed onto the sofa, my bare feet carefully sinking into the space behind him, then sat on the back of the sofa. I leaned into him, and pushed with all my might, pleading with him to move and get off. It must have been such a funny sight, but if my dad had walked in he wouldn't have found it funny.

No matter what I said to him, he would always have thought I got him up there on purpose and was just fooling around. Of course I wasn't that daft, and wouldn't have put the pooch in such a position, but back then it wouldn't have mattered, he would never have believed him.

You can imagine the relief then when Sammy suddenly decided of his own free will to get down. Either he had had enough of my pushing and prodding him, or he just felt sorry for me, but whatever it was he had decided to get down. He barely got two feet and flopped onto the cold floor, between the rug and the large open fire.

I was out of breath and still giggling. It was one of the funniest things I have ever seen from a dog, being so lazy and so wilful, that more than anything is a reminder to me of what a character he really was.

So began the weekend, and I knew that come Monday things would be different. It would be school, and more like my life at home. I was certainly determined to make the most of what I had left, and especially with those two dogs.

CHAPTER FIVE

The best thing about being in Kenya was that waking up you were almost always met with lovely warmth and tons of sunshine. It meant you could be free to go out and do as you pleased, and even better being in a new country there was so much to explore and so many new things to see. The only times this wasn't the case was in the rainy season, like the monsoon season, when it would be cold, dark and overcast, endlessly raining Some of the rain then was insane in its strength, but it was also a sight to behold.

That weekend it was amazing, so warm, the skies so blue, endlessly, as if we were encircled by it in our own little universe. For the poorest around us it was one small saving grace, but at that age I had little understanding of it, or what their lives were like. We lived right next to a town or such abject poverty, and it seemed our lives just went on as if there wasn't a problem.

I got up on the Saturday morning and the first thing I came up with was to have some fun with the dogs. I jumped up, got dressed into a very baggy t-shirt and some jeans I had grown out of but still insisted on wearing. I wore the same old trainers. Every time I put them on I think more of them broke off, until the sole on the bottom of one of them hung off like Sammy's flappy tongue.

I was just about to go outside when mum came from the kitchen and caught me. "You can't go out until you've had breakfast."

I shrugged and went to get something. "I'll have a steak I think," I said, because meat like that in Kenya was so cheap, and it seemed to be the only thing we ever had.

"No you won't, you'll have cereal like a normal person," she insisted, so I did. I got a bowl of porridge, added cold water and went to sit at the dining room table without thinking about heating it up. At that age I didn't even know you were supposed to, and I think mum just let it happen as she thought it would be funny. Back then and being there we didn't have a microwave so it meant always using the cooker, something I had no clue about. I didn't even know washing machines were a thing, I was so cosseted.

I put the bowl on the table, sat down and lifted my spoon, but before I could take my first mouthful, I was shocked to see almost instantly, right next to me were both dogs, sitting there all proud, looking at me as if I were the bone this time. Again I just laughed at them, their timing was impeccable, like a double act perfectly in sync whenever the possibility of food arose. I didn't give them any, and didn't enjoy it anyway, because it needed heating. No way would I go do that.

"I'm just gonna take the dogs for a walk," I said getting up from the table. Nobody answered, so I figured it must be alright. Neither dog had a collar, and I doubted either dog had ever been taken in properly as a pet before, there was nothing about them which would suggest otherwise. No matter, because they were with us then, we would provide all the love they ever needed.

As Shrink didn't have a collar, I had to go and search the place for some rope or string. There wasn't a lot in the house as we hadn't been there very long, and hardly bought anything, but the people employing my dad had made sure we had most of what was needed. I looked in the bathroom, then the kitchen, looking in all of the cupboards. I was bit shocked how little there was there, it seemed like the place had never been lived in. Then I went into the garden and finally found some cord which had been used to fasten some of the plants in the garden up. It looked liked it was strong enough, but I didn't want to put that around Shrink's neck, so had to come up with something ingenious.

As I eventually got both dogs fastened up to my satisfaction, I opened the front door and walked out, but before I could get anywhere, my mum caught me.

"Hold on, what are you doing?" she asked, as my dad had finally got up and joined her.

"Where are you going?" Dad asked.

I looked at them both quite innocently. "Just taking the dogs out for a walk," I said.

Both of them looked at me as if I were a little mad. I had tied some of the cord around Sammy's waist and front legs, in a kind of harness, but unable to find anything suitable for Shrink I had taken off the baggy t-shirt I had been wearing, put it on him, and tied some of the cord to it so I could control him. There I was, wearing jeans that were too small for me, floppy soled training shoes and no top on. Sammy was stood looking unhappy at the idea of being walked, and Shrink could hardly be seen at all because he was buried under the shirt which was twice as big as he was.

Nobody laughed. I think they weren't sure whether I was being serious or not. I was.

I got the first inclination that something was wrong when Shrink tried to walk ahead and one of the sleeves dropped and he tripped on it, nearly falling over. We wouldn't have got far.

"You can't take Sammy out, he's too big for you, and probably won't want to walk far," dad said. I got that, as daft as I was I wasn't surprised by that idea.

"You can't go out without a top on, you'll burn in this sun," Mum said. She had a habit of telling me how hot the sun got by midday there, and that going out meant inevitable instant death. Even if she had been right I wouldn't have taken any notice of her.

"He needs a better collar," Dad said, looking at Shrink. It was like the ten commandments, where I had all these rules, but then looking back as funny as it was, I wasn't very sensible.

So back to the drawing board I went. I went indoors and got a new t-shirt on, plus lashings of suntan lotion. Sammy was unfastened and allowed to go and hide, away from me, while my dad did his thing and went and get an old leather belt he didn't need. He was a dab hand at making things, which was the nature of his job, and did an amazing job of creating a small but perfectly formed collar for Shrink. We had nothing else for a lead, but he doubled up the cord to make it extra strong.

I took hold of the new lead, beckoned Shrink and went to leave.

"Be careful, don't go far, don't go for long, don't talk to strangers," mum insisted, at which dad once again caught her attention, reminding her of the need to let me grow up. She was right in a way, being in a new country, so new to us, and with such different people, not to mention the potential language barrier. I had no intention of going far, but I couldn't resist taking one of the dogs for a walk. It felt like a real adventure.

I took hold of Shrink's lead and walked up the small drive, opened the large gates and out onto the roadway outside. There was a small dirt garden bit at the front of the gates, a bit of tarmac to the road and then the main road went left and right. There was a huge rock face at the opposite side of the road, and the houses being on a hill, the further right you went the steeper the hill became. To the left the road wound around the estate and was the route to Nairobi city centre. As we had driven left to go into the city several times already, I chose to go right, to see what was there.

Being so high up on a hill, you could see everything below, and it was quite spectacular, especially on an evening with the sun setting low behind the hills. The sky would turn a burnt orange colour and any clouds would slowly dissipate away like smoke drifting away from a fire. It was still quite early, and so the sun wasn't fully risen, and the air not too hot to make walking a chore. Shrink seemed quite at ease by my side, and I was feeling really good about things. I just plodded alongside the smooth tarmac road and headed down the hill, wondering where it would take me and what I would see.

"Hey," a voice called out, catching my attention, but I was a little wary of speaking to anyone I didn't know, still finding myself in the new country. I ignored it at first, and just carried on walking.

"What's your name?" someone asked, and I suddenly felt all hot and flushed. I really began to wonder how good an idea it might be to go walking along after all.

I had two choices, to either look and answer, or just turn back and go home. Shrink made the choice for me, stopping to lift his leg to have a wee. Right by the side of the road, near to where I had been called from. It might have been fate because it made a real difference to my time there, good and bad.

I finally looked up, to see a young boy stood over near a gate, and beside him someone a little older. The older one was taller and kept tugging at the small boy's shirt, as if to say stop.

"What's your name?" the small boy asked again. I felt no small amount of relief, as well as being pleased to see someone like me. I told them my name, in the coy way young often do, without much emotion or giving anything away.

"I'm Simon," the young boy said. He was wearing shorts that were far too big for him, which seemed to be an ongoing trait for young people in Africa. It seemed that the moment you got anywhere hot, the solution for adults was to put all their children in shorts as if to proclaim they had arrived, they had made it to a hot country and needed to show it.

Simon was short, not just because he was young, he must have been around seven, but he was short naturally, and always seemed so. He wore a t-shirt like I had, several sizes too large, and was covered in mud. Whatever they had been up to, they had been having fun doing it. His hair was a large cascading mop of wispy blonde. He wore sandals, which I later found were very much in keeping with the style of the whole family.

I looked up at the other boy, who had until then remained silent. He just stood there looking at me suspiciously, like I was some kind of lion about to pounce and eat them both. By the way he acted you wouldn't think I was so young as well. He looked around ten or eleven, had much darker hair than the other, and was also wearing shorts. He wore a stripy t-shirt with a picture of a dog on it, which suggested to me he liked dogs. It would be a good thing, because we would have something in common.

"What's your name?" I asked, looking at the older boy. He didn't reply, just continuing to look at me in a way which suggested things wouldn't go too well. That first impression of him turned out to be right, and he and I never really got on.

"His name is Kelly?" the young boy answered, at which the older boy nudged him, begrudging him for daring to tell anyone anything about him.

Regardless of how he behaved, he did look at Shrink, which broke the ice between us all. "What's that?" he asked.

"What's what?" I asked, because it never occurred to me that anyone would refer to Shrink as a *that*.

Kelly pointed to Shrink. "That," he said abruptly. In most circumstances I would have ignored him and walked away, but not knowing anyone, I didn't want to lose out on being friends with someone.

"That's my dog, Shrink," I said.

46

"Funny looking dog," Kelly said. I felt like saying something about how he looked, but before I could Simon interrupted us.

"Why is he called Shrink?" Simon asked, squinting, which he often did even when it wasn't sunny. He had some interesting characteristics, but he was always a nice unassuming person, unlike Kelly who always seemed to have an agenda.

I explained my reasons, and told them about Sammy. I explained what had happened on the sofa and both laughed at it. It was a good way to get to know each other.

"You live here?" I asked. They were stood in front of a single story house, much like ours, with a large gate in front of it.

"Yep," Kelly said.

"Mum and dad are teachers, we've been here ages," Simon explained. They looked and seemed much like we were, but I could see from the small open top car in the driveway they were a bit more settled. As I was looking I saw a dog wander past the main gate, followed by another. They were a mid brown colour, very much alike, but were wandering around as if looking for something.

"Are they your pets?" I asked. It was the first thing that popped into my head, because they didn't look too friendly.

"No," Simon said.

"Yes," Kelly replied.

"Right, which is it?" I asked, feeling pretty amused by their sideshow. I liked Simon, he was pretty honest with me and always straightforward. I could tell straight away Kelly had a problem with me, which ultimately never went away.

"They are our dogs, and they're our pets too," Kelly said, only he was looking at Simon now. As he spoke he nudged him in the arm, giving him an annoyed look. Simon shoved him back harder.

"No they're not, they just look after us," Simon insisted. Kelly shoved back, too hard as Simon fell over, immediately bursting into tears.

"Mummy," Simon shouted, trying to pick himself up. Kelly didn't seem the least bit bothered by his brother's knee bleeding, or the amount of noise he was making. All I could see was Shrink beginning to circle nervously. It was obvious he didn't like groups of young people.

"I'd better get going," I said, but neither were interested in me anymore. As I began to walk away a short, blonde haired woman came out of the house, quickly making her way over to the boys. I turned away and walked off, deciding it was better to not get involved.

Shrink seemed to calm down a lot once we got walking. I could see the way his little legs were bouncing as we walked that he was enjoying it.

As we walked further down, the road changed, as the tarmac ran out and it became more of a stretch of hard flat mud. The housing estate ended too, as from that point on it seemed long stretches of banana plants, large trees and bushes. People were milling around here and there. Though I had been there a while, I could never get used to seeing people wearing the same kind of clothes as me, but that so many of them had no shoes or socks on. It never occurred to me back then that few did because they couldn't afford them.

Shrink suddenly began to struggle against the lead, to the point where I became afraid he was going to break free and run off. I really panicked. I figured if he got away there was no way I would be able to catch him. I bent down on one knee and tried comforting him, but he was still so agitated. Instead of fighting against him, I just decided to go with it and see where he took me. Immediately he charged forwards, dragging me along, off the road, onto the mud path and then down a bank. Down there the embankment had literally broken away, as it seemed some kind of concrete storm drain had broken, taking a large part of the mud hills with it.

A big problem there at the time was soil erosion, with such long periods of dry weather, followed by heavy rains, soil would wash away, often causing a lot of damage. Water flowed out from a large pipe. It was actually frightening to see, because its power and intensity was frankly ferocious. This one major outlet was from a broken pipe under the estate, and pure water was surging out from it.

Again Shrink kept pulling, each time I allowed him to go a little bit further, but I was terrified of going too close to it and falling in. The water had created a large, deep trench as it spilled out into the open fields further away. Several people, mostly women were dipping bowls and tubs into it to collect water, and one woman had even gone further down and was actually washing clothes in it. People are ingenious to say the least, no matter where they're from.

The bank down was quite steep, and very muddy, but as the water flowed out further on it was much better, flatter land and safe. Of course this wouldn't occur to a dog, certainly not Shrink, as he insisted on getting close to it immediately. Just as he got to the edge, my foot gave way and I slipped over onto my backside. I think others there looking at me probably thought I was an idiot, and I was, being led around by such a small dog, but for all his diminutive size he was still very strong. Unfortunately as I fell my left foot kicked out, catching Shrink right in the bottom, sending him flailing out into the water. I was so shocked at falling that as he went flying I dropped the lead.

Splash he went right into this torrent of water and I cried out like a baby. I just panicked, thinking all was lost. Typical me to get a dog and straight away lose him, worse, by kicking him away like a rugby ball.

My first instincts were to jump right in after him. I could swim but not that great. I stood up, went to jump but someone grabbed hold of my arm, hard, dragging me back. I looked back to see a tall, slender man, scruffy shocked hair, wearing a worn bright green shirt and baggy cotton trousers. He wore no shoes,

49

and looked to be in his twenties. His eyes were wide, as shocked at my thinking of going in as I was to see Shrink fly off.

"No, no go in there," he insisted in broken English.

"But my dog, he fell in," I said, by which time I was almost crying.

The spectacle of that water outflow was hard to comprehend, it took rainfall from other parts in a long pipe under the estate, and acted as a bypass for all of it. When it had rained heavy the flow was clearly incredibly powerful, and dangerous.

I looked up trying to see Shrink as the man let go of my arm. Far from being unpredictable in Kenya, nearly all of the people I met there were kind and very friendly. I never did meet anyone who wasn't decent with me.

"Come on..." he pointed, away from the outbreak of water. Of course if I had kept a clear head I would have done just that, imagined Shrink flowing down to an easier part to access and going straight there for him. My mind was just a wild clash of speculation and fear. I was terrified, not just of the water but for my dog.

The man jumped off the muddy bank and ran away further down, looking across the edge. Finally getting a grip of what I was doing, I came to my senses sufficiently that I could follow him. I was trying to look out, as tears streamed down my face.

"Shrink!" I called out, which must certainly have confused others who were around there. I can't imagine anyone immediately thinking that was a dog's name, rather some strange claim for something to shrink down. I didn't really care what people thought, I was just horrified at what had happened.

Every few yards the man stopped and looked in, leaning over as best he could, looking all around. I just stopped with him, hoping and praying for a miracle.

The further up we went the easier the flow of water was and less aggressive. Right up it became something of a river, then in the distance more of a steady stream.

I felt completely lost, so utterly broken inside that he had drowned and it was all my fault. I could never live with myself.

"Shrink," I said again, feebly, just walking along like a zombie. I was totally empty.

"There," the man said suddenly, pointing. I looked up, in disbelief, at something in the distance. No way was it him, impossible. The man broke out into a run, dropping quickly into the water, which by then was thankfully only knee deep. He waded across, grabbed something up in his arms and turned back to me.

I was having a hard time seeing. Tears and self pity had blurred my vision for a moment, but I struggled hard to keep my eyes open, to stare at what he was doing, wide eyed even if it hurt so that I could see what had caught his attention.

The man leaned over in the water, picked up Shrink and held him in his arms. He looked back at me, but from his expression I feared the worse. I wasn't so brave as to just jump in, so I went to the bank, sat down, leaned my feet over and dropped gently in. It went up to my waist and as burning as the sun way, the water was freezing. It took my breath away harshly, but I was determined to get to him. The man waded closer to me, holding him tightly. Shrink didn't move.

The moment I got to him, all I could see was this little dog, his fur all matted, laying as if lifeless in the man's arms. I was shaking by then, and not just with the cold, but for fear of what had happened, sheer hurt from it all. I leaned my hand out, daring not touch him, but just as I was about to touch his head, he lifted it a little, and blinked at me. I laughed in between the tears, so much relief, but happiness that this lovely little doggy was still with me.

"Go," the man said, holding Shrink tightly, but pointing with his other hand that we should leave. It was a good idea, it was bitterly cold.

We got to the bank and I climbed out, trying to take Shrink, but the man was too busy climbing out to think of handing him over. We both stood there dripping, looking at each other. For a

51

moment I genuinely thought he was just going to take this little dog and walk away.

"Did you fall in?" a voice asked. I turned to see a young woman stood next to me. The man said something in Swahili to her, which I never did find out what it was. The young woman looked shocked by what she had seen.

"You must be careful in these places," she said. Her accent was a beautiful Kenyan tone, but with such perfect English with it. Her eyes were so clear, she looked a lovely person and the care and concern in her manner was typical of how many were in the times I was there.

"It was an accident, I..." I began to say, but I felt sick with the worry I had felt, not to mention embarrassment of it. It was then that I learned something about myself, that somehow I felt superior to them, even though here I was a stranger in their country, I felt somehow I was better than them, more money, more power, better in every way. The truth was I only learned that about myself in the moment that I had proven to myself that it wasn't the case, that we were no different, no better, and for me, I was more inclined than anyone to do something stupid.

Shrink actually turned his head up as I held him, to look at me, and for that moment I genuinely thought he was sharing their thoughts about me: stupid boy. He was soaked. Even though it was warm out, the water had been freezing. He was such a little thing that he had no fat on him to protect him from the worst of the elements. I don't think I could have felt any worse than I did.

I turned and looked at the man who had helped me. "Thanks," I said, realising I had learned a lot about the people around me. So many of them were so poor, and yet they were more often than not good and decent people, which I guess I had never expected. I looked at the woman and she smiled at me. I think she must have seen from my reaction that I had learned something. Whatever it was, it has always stayed with me.

Sheepishly I walked off, still holding Shrink, as if I should let him go and he would disappear back into the water again. I knew full well that if it had been an actual river I might never have seen him again, that it was only because it was only a broken pipe spilling out such huge amounts of water that here he was, still with me. I really felt like crying, but being the age I was, I didn't any more. I didn't want to look foolish, not in front of others, but to myself.

As I walked slowly back to the house, I passed the house with the two boys. Simon was nowhere to be seen, but Kelly was outside again. He had that same scowl on his face that he always seemed to have, which didn't exactly endear him to me.

"What happened to him?" Kelly asked me. For a moment I was gladdened that someone seemed to be concerned, not someone I had expected either.

"He fell in some fast flowing water down there, some people helped me get him back," I said, pleased to have someone else to tell it to, a kind of release, as much my emotions over it than anything else.

Kelly suddenly burst out laughing, pointing his finger at us both. Shrink looked as sorry for himself as I felt, but we were both wet and unhappy. It was the last thing I needed. I never said another word to him, but walked on, still holding shrink, listening to that boy laugh his head off like some kind of hyena. It wasn't very nice, and unfortunately was a taste of things to come with him. Sadly for me there weren't any others close by that I could get to know. Stupid as it sounds it never occurred to me to hang out around African children. I guess I figured it might not be safe, but back then I didn't know any better.

As we got closer to the house, with it in sight, Shrink must have seen it and began to squirm quickly. At first I tried extra hard to hold onto him, not wanting to allow him out of my sight again. No way was I going to let that happen again, ever.

I kept a tight hold of his leash, but he strained and pulled, until we got to the gate and I opened it, then he broke free of my grip and ran off into the garden and around the back. When

I go to the front door it was locked, so I went round the side of the house, following where Shrink had gone, to see he was sat at mum's feet, as she and my dad were in the padded recliners, drinks jug on the table, enjoying the sun.

Mum had a concerned look on her face, but I could see dad was waiting for an excuse to do what Kelly did. Surprisingly he never did laugh, I expect he must have seen the upset look on my face and decided not to.

"What happened?" my mum asked, looking me up and down. She could see I was drenched still. The sun had begun to dry me a little, but my clothes were muddy and my hair still damp.

"Shrink fell in some water down at the bottom, and I had to get in to get him," I replied, still waiting for dad to have his fun moment at my expense.

"Was he too strong for you, Shrink?" my dad asked. He couldn't help himself. He didn't laugh about it, but I could see from the look on his face he had found it amusing. It was a change anyway, from when I was younger, because back then he would never have laughed, he would have been angry about it.

Mum didn't wait for me to reply. "Go get changed and come and sit outside with us," she said. I think she was just glad I was back again. I can understand her worry back then, but all that was hurt was my pride. Shrink meanwhile had gone onto the grass and laid down, licking his paws. He looked up into the sun, quickly drying, and back to normal. I guess it had been a little adventure for him, but for me it was a reminder that I was still very young in such a country where anything can and did happen.

CHAPTER SIX

The matter was quickly forgotten, but I wouldn't be in any rush to go out again. Shrink duly avoided me for a while, as if I were to blame for his woes. He dried and subsequently licked himself clean, and I left him to it. Besides there was another dog, and he was less cat like, and much more horse like, big, fat, slow, but loving with it. He was like a grumpy old man, that didn't say much but he certainly had a presence about him that endeared him to everyone who ever met him.

It stayed light that time of year, and being so warm my parents both stayed sat outside. I had gone in and just sat on the living room carpet with Sammy. He didn't have the energy to do much, but his tail flapped hard on the matt when I rubbed him. He rolled over onto this back and I rubbed his belly, and the more I did the more his tail went and the eventually so his back leg kicked in doing his bicycle bit. When we first got him he was very dusty, but since being bathed he smelled much better, and you could see how black his coat was. He had a bit of grey around his muzzle, but otherwise, apart from being fat you couldn't see why he was so lethargic. I guess he was just a lazy dog.

As usual there was nothing on television, other than musical programmes from the seventies or African soaps, which being in Swahili I had no clue what they were about. I hoped to learn in time, but of course I was in no rush.

I suddenly felt the need to go use the bathroom, so got up quickly to go and to my surprise Sammy rolled right over and jumped up. He moved so fast, I had no idea he was even capable of it. I think my rubbing his tummy must have impressed him. I went off, up the steps and he followed me, which was a nice surprise.

As I walked down the hall, it had begun to get a little dark, but I could see well enough. Suddenly a dark thing flittered across the hall floor. I felt my heart leap and I jumped. Sammy must have seen it too, because he hunched over, staring at this dark thing scattering around. I had no idea what it was, but I could and did imagine all sorts. I was terrified, imagining that some strange creature might do the unimaginable and jump up at me and bite my face off. Of course I was being daft, but then at that age, in such circumstances I had no idea what to do.

I leaned my arm out, more out of instinct than anything else, not daring to move in case it came towards me. I had socks on but no shoes and feared the worst. Somehow I managed to flick on a light switch and everything became clear, which I instantly regretted. It must have been the biggest spider I have ever seen in my life. There is a place in Nairobi where spiders and snakes and all sorts can be seen as exhibitions, but all dead and pinned to the wall in cases, but nightmares, it was bigger than anything from there, as big as a man's hand. It was very dark and covered in fur, but no other markings I could see. What terrified me the most was how fast it was, flitting across the floor so quickly you would think it was on wheels.

I figured to go and get my dad, he would deal with it, but before I could turn to do so, Sammy decided it would be an opportunity to show he did know how to play after all and this spider would be his new play thing. Being all his life in Africa, he wasn't daft. Sure he must have known about dangers, and had the instincts to avoid them, because he had survived this long, but right then and there that all seemed to fly right out of the window.

He jumped, front paws springing up, and at it, landing right next to it. The next thing he actually tried to pick it up, snapping at it, mouth open, and actually caught it, sending it flying as he released it. At first I thought he was being protective, but then I could see when he began running, or trotting as he mostly did back and forth, his tail wagging, he really did seem to think it was funny. I wanted to go and get my mum and dad, but I was afraid if I left Sammy might bite it again and get bitten himself and by the time we got back he would be dead. I panicked.

"Sammy, no," I shouted, clapping my hands. I don't think he was a dog who was raised to answer the call of anyone speaking English, but I had no idea how to call him. All I had learned was to say Jambo for hello and Kwaheri for saying goodbye, I hadn't got to the part where I said yes or no in African. Naturally Sammy ignored me, carrying on playing. I was in a state, but the second time in a day and with the second of our dogs. The way it was going with dogs I wasn't sure they would last the week around me.

I got the feeling the spider was not enjoying it one little bit. It seemed so large and so quick, I knew it could react if it wanted to but it just seemed to want to get away. It scuttled across the floor towards the other side of the hall then tried to get away in the opposite direction to us. Sammy bounded towards it, snapped at it once again then dropped it, before grabbing at it again. Only this time he shook his head, licking himself, and from the look on his muzzle I could see he really didn't enjoy it. Fearing he had been stung or bitten, I just had to do something.

It was probably the daftest thing I have ever done, before or since, but all I could think about was Sammy dying, so I just went and leaned over, pushing Sammy away, and grabbed at the spider. I picked it up by one of its legs, feeling a total sense of terror coursing through me. I was horrified. I've never been too bothered by spiders before, or even now, but it was so big and moved in the kind of way I had seen in films just as they ate people. I knew very well that wasn't true, but instincts are tough things to overcome. The spider struggled and wriggled in my hand, but I remained as gentle as I could, holding onto it.

Sammy just looked up at me, eyes wide, as if it were a tennis ball and I was going to throw it so he could get it in a game of catch. It was all fun for him, he was too daft to realize what the problems was. Maybe though, it was me that was the daft one, because I had panicked, and he seemed quite relaxed and happy about it.

I went as fast as I could to the front door, unlocked it and opened it before throwing it as hard as I could. This little furry bundle of black flew out, into the rockery on to some plants. It landed softer than I had expected, before scurrying away.

Straight away I slammed the door, as my mind insisted on flooding my vision with images of it fighting to get back in at us. In reality it would be going the opposite way, thankful it had survived, but I was too scared and out of breath to think like that.

I locked the door for good measure, ignored the terribly disappointed look on Sammy's face that I had taken away his play toy and thrown it outside, and went out back to my parents.

"You'll never believe it," I said dramatically.

Both of my parents looked at me, in mock surprise, but clearly not taking me seriously.

"What, what?" my mum asked hurriedly. Ignoring their response, I just carried on, incredulous at my own bravery.

"There was a huge spider in the hallway," I explained, still feeling breathless.

"What, a spider?" my mum asked. At least she got how awful it was, I wanted to explain to her just how awful.

"Huge did you say?" my dad asked again, in his typical mocking tones. I ignored him.

"It was black, covered in hair, and Sammy was trying to bite it."

"Oh Sammy, you brave thing," mum replied, looking directly at Sammy as if all he needed was a cape and he could fly.

"No, he was trying to play with it," I tried to explain.

"So it was a huge deadly dangerous spider, but he wanted to play with it," dad said. I could tell he was goading me but I refused to rise to it.

Mum knew better, she was shocked. She didn't like spiders at all, which made coming to live in a country full of them just a little bit odd.

"Where is it?" Mum asked, moving forward in her chair. I could see she wanted to recoil in horror, as if it might come running out of the house any moment and she would have to get away.

"I picked it up, and threw it in the front garden, before it had a chance to do anything to Sammy."

That did the trick, as both of my parents gave me a look of absolute shock.

"You picked it up?" my dad asked, finally dropping the pretence of bravery. I knew he wouldn't have done it, though he would probably have stood on it.

"You shouldn't do that, you never know what could happen," Mum said, more worried than afraid now.

"I'm fine, I threw it outside, I was careful, and me and Sammy are fine now."

Mum was shaking her head. I could see my dad felt the same, but he wasn't one for dwelling on things, good or bad.

"Oh, the thought of spiders, drives me mad," Mum said. I almost burst out laughing, given the circumstances, but instead my natural ego kicked in.

"It's ok, if you see one, give me a call and I'll be right there to deal with it," I said, trying to sound brave. In reality I was still shaking from it and felt sick over it. My dad just looked at me, with a kind of knowing look, but I would like to see him deal with one as humanely as I did.

Panic over, we all went back indoors. Sammy followed me, making me wonder if perhaps he thought I still had the spider in my hand and might throw it for him.

We ate a nice tea, big piece of beef, potatoes and veg, and as it was late all decided to go to bed. I got changed, and made sure to get washed after such a messed up day, then into bed. I was proud of myself, and couldn't stop thinking how quickly I had acted, how brave I had been without thinking about it.

I pulled up my covers, turned over and set out to dream about my adventures as the *spider hunter*.

Normally the only thing that affected my sleep there was the heat, as during the night it was often unbearable and we had no air conditioning. That night was different. I woke up to find it pitch black outside, but most importantly, I was struggling to breathe. In all of my life I have never had asthma, but it felt like I had imagined it to be. My chest was tight, and I just couldn't get my breath. I tried sitting up, and thought about opening the windows, but I didn't have the strength. All of the windows on the house had large bars all over them, so opening a window wasn't something I wanted to do. I just waited, hoping as I woke a bit it would pass.

Usually I would fall back asleep quickly, but not that time. My breathing was so tight I couldn't stay there, so got up and walked out, down the hall to the living room. I flicked the light switch on, only to see Sammy sprawled out on the sofa again, snoring like a tractor. Mum had brought Shrink back in and he was curled up in a tight little ball in the centre of the rug. They seemed happy enough, and Sammy hadn't been bothered by anything, just me.

It got so bad, I knew I wouldn't be able to sleep it off, I had to say something. I walked back down the hall to my parents room.

"Mum," I said quietly. I always called her when young, but hadn't needed to for so long. Dad wasn't the kind of person who appreciated being woken up. Ever.

No reply, so I called again a little louder. I knew it was going to be a problem, because I could feel my breathing getting worse than ever, so much I thought I was going to pass out. In the end I turned on the hall light, tapping on their door, which was partly open.

"Mum," I said louder than ever.

"What," mum said suddenly, sitting right up. She was like that, always ready to act quickly if she thought something was wrong.

"I don't feel well, I can't breathe," I said, struggling to speak at all. Apart from not having the breath to do it, my voice rasped as I spoke, as if I had inhaled a lot of smoke and my throat was closed up and sore.

Dad woke up by that point and the two of them got out of bed, clearly concerned at the sound coming from me, as I sounded like a diesel engine.

Dad came round the other side of mum, looking at me intently. He was clearly very concerned.

"What's up?" I asked, a bit of an obvious question given how I sounded.

"Your face," dad said, and I was fully expecting him to say something witty and sarcastic at my expense. The fact that he didn't alarmed me, because from the look on his face he was very concerned. One thing about him you could say was a positive, that he never really panicked about things. His concern was always met with action and dealing with things. This time he looked lost.

"Why, what's wrong with my face?" I struggled to ask, but my breathing was so bad I could hardly utter the words.

Mum came round him and looked at me. She looked even more concerned, if that were possible. They looked at each other, then back at me.

"Have you eaten anything, been snacking on anything?" my mum asked. I thought about it and shook my head. Often with it being so warm I would usually drink pop at night, and hardly ever ate supper, so whatever was wrong, it couldn't be anything I ate.

"What's wrong, I just can't breathe very well, but why are you looking at me like that?" I asked, and was more worried about how they looked at me than anything else.

"Your face is all swollen, and bloodshot," mum said, which really did make me panic. I went straight to the bathroom and looked in the mirror. My face was unrecognisable, all puffy blotches, some large, all very red with a strong point of red in the centre of each. Mum took hold of my arm, and it was clear I was covered in this, all over my body.

"Oh no," I said dramatically.

Dad of course reacted calmly. Even if he felt panicked he never showed it. Whether that was a lack of emotion and compassion or whether he was just like it to keep us calm was debatable.

"OK, we'll have to go find a hospital," he said. I was glad he was going to do this, because I had no idea what to do or where to go. My impression of Africa prior to getting there was that I didn't even know if they had such things as hospitals, such was my naivety back then.

We all dressed and then I followed my parents down the hall. As we got to the top of the few steps above the living room, I noticed Sammy still laid out right across the sofa. My dad took one look at him, then looked at me as if to say he gave up trying with him. Of course he wouldn't, he would do something about it later, but he had bigger fish to fry than persistent dogs.

By the time we got into the car I noticed it was four in the morning, and still very dark out. Dad had actually managed to get in touch with someone from work and they had told us where to go, a private clinic somewhere a short drive away. He headed there, and by the time we got there I was like the Michelin man, all swollen up, coarse heavy breathing, blotches all over, a real state. I felt alright, except for my breathing.

The clinic was small, with two nurses and an Asian doctor. He called me in, with my parents to a small area screened off. I took off my t-shirt and he looked at me, but it seemed he knew straight away what it was.

"He has been bitten, most likely by a spider, and suffered an allergic reaction," the doctor said, looking mostly at my dad.

A thought hit me as to what might have happened, but I was never one to drop myself in it if I didn't have to.

"Is it serious?" mum asked.

"Well if it was very serious, he might well be unconscious now, so the fact that he can walk in means it is treatable," the doctor explained. I felt a huge sense of relief, to say the least.

"I'll give you some tablets for him to take, and see how it goes for a few days, and if any problems, come back and we will take another look."

All I could think then was I wanted to go home and get in bed. My parents paid for the tablets and thanked them, and we all left, back home again.

"So you did get bit by that spider after all," my dad said, without looking at me as he drove us home. There went any chance I had of bluffing what might have caused it.

"It might not have been that one, could have been a different one," I said hopefully.

"Well just goes to show you, don't go picking up spiders," Mum said, completely ignoring my attempted to excuse myself and deflect blame.

When we got back, Sammy was still laid out on the sofa, hardly having even moved to breathe. Shrink met us at the door, sort of wagging his tail. It was so long and pointy he never could really do much with it, but it was nice to see him try. Immediately I stepped in and smiled, arms open to welcome him. He took one look at me, sniffed me and turned and ran off, down the steps into the living room and hid behind the sofa. It must be true what they say about dogs knowing when you're ill.

"Nice, thanks Shrink," I said. I took some tablets and headed back to bed.

"Oh, one more thing," my dad said, turning back as he headed for the bedroom. I looked up, feeling tired and not particularly interested. "Until you get better, you won't be able to go to school," he said, disappearing to bed. I just stood there a moment, wishing I had the voice to scream out. If there was one positive to come from being bitten by a spider in Africa, it was the chance to miss school. Now all I needed was to convince Shrink to come back to me again.

CHAPTER SEVEN

As it turned out, being ill in order to avoid school wasn't all it was cracked up to be. I ended up permanently sat in a chair, either indoors or outside, struggling to breathe, covered in lumps, without any energy and feeling sick all the time. I doubted school would be any worse. At least I had the two dogs there to keep me company.

The worst part was there was nothing to do, no games to play, no television that I would like, no magazines or things to read, other than those days, weeks or months that were out of date. Mum stayed indoors and dad had gone into work a day early to meet people, but that Sunday dragged.

Eventually I just got tired of doing nothing, except sitting and drinking. I could barely eat because my throat was closed up. Nobody knew what had gotten at me, but it seemed just a part of living in such a country. The attitude was if you were still alive then it wasn't that bad.

Sat there in the afternoon, I clapped my hands together and beckoned Sammy. I was outside and of course no way was he going to come running out there in that heat. I had a thing covering me, like a cloth parasol, so I didn't burn, but Sammy being deep black coated never liked too much sun.

I tried clapping again, but no luck, trying to call his name some more. "Sammy, got a bone for you," I rasped. Out he popped through the door as if by magic. Of all the things he would understand me to say, it had to be that word, bone, he just knew what it was. He wasn't daft though, not like shrink, as he stood by the door and looked at me. The moment I saw him I smiled at him and clapped as best I could. He took one look, noticed straight away the absence of a bone, and turned to head back in. He could be really impossible at times.

I thought about calling or clapping for Shrink, but so far he had carried on hiding from me, possibly afraid of how I looked, all bubbly and sounding odd when I breathed and spoke. So I struggled up, making my way back indoors. There was Sammy, now laid on the cool wooden floor, still spread out as if he were made of butter. Mum was sat in one of the large chairs, watching an old Val Doonican special, entirely engrossed in it. I just sat next to Sammy on the floor, and nobody noticed me. It was as if I were a ghost and had just drifted in unseen.

As I sat a moment listening to Irish crooning on the TV, I spotted something out of the corner of my eye. My first reaction was panic, because it looked small and black, and I had this terrible fear that the spider was coming back, looking for me again. I sat there on the floor, frozen to the spot, looking at this small black thing poked out from behind the sofa. I tensed myself, as sick as I was feeling I was definitely going to up and run if it came scurrying out. Just as I was about to leap up, so I saw a shiny wet nose prod through, little whiskers trembling, as Shrink leaned slowly out, as if he were playing hide and seek. He had never been one to make much eye contact, but for the first time since we had got him he did, giving me the most cheeky look you can imagine.

Mum was oblivious to it. I think she was too wrapped up in Val Doonican. I smiled a lot at Shrink, seeing how cautious and yet playful he was. I didn't move, or hold out a hand to him, just waited and watched. He stepped forward a little more so I could see his little paws delicately treading on the carpet, ever so slowly, all the time his eyes focused on me. I could tell he wanted to come to me, but he just seemed so afraid that I might do something to him, or that he might catch what I had. Perhaps he had experienced something bad with spiders before, or just natural dog instincts. Whatever it was it had made him very cool towards me.

I decided to try something, and so leaned sideways, gradually slumping over, allowing myself to easily drop to the floor, without using my hands or any sudden movements, until I was laid on my side, all the while still looking at Shrink. He stopped a moment when I moved, but as I lay there, he began to move again, but he didn't blink, just wide eyed as he moved. I think he wanted to come to me, but was wary in case something happened to him. I guess life hadn't always been kind to him, and he wasn't too used to good people such as us.

Shrink didn't stop then, he just gradually walked towards me as I lay there, his pads clipping on the wooden floor. As small as he was, he was stood right over my head, leaning down to me, his little black shiny nose just an inch or two away, eyes staring at me. He did so in such a kind and playful way, I just wanted to grab hold of him and give him a big hug. I didn't

65

because I was afraid that if I did anything too abrupt he might run away and perhaps never come back to me, not in the same way.

What he did next surprised me more than anything. He pushed into me a little, then a little closer, and gently nudged into me, until he was curled up, partly in my arms, and partly resting on my stomach. The top of his head was just below my nose, and he smelt all warm and sun fresh. I was a lovely moment, so gentle and sweet. I was so enamoured by it that I just laid there with him, slowly and carefully putting my right arm across him, until my hand settled on his coat, resting on him, feeling his slow breathing beneath my hand.

I couldn't recall what happened next, because it was so comfortable that I drifted quickly off to sleep.

*

"What's going on there?" I heard someone say. I say heard, but I was so warm and at peace that I could barely hear anything, drifting in and out of sleep.

"You can't sleep down there," a booming voice said. It was typical of my dad, so lacking in care at times. Fair enough, I was right in the way of the back door and nobody could get past, but his voice was so loud and abrupt I jumped, and so did Shrink.

I looked up to see dad standing over me. I was feeling pretty miffed about it, not to mention so sleepy, but then I noticed he was stood there with a very large double cone, full of white ice cream and chocolate flakes in it.

"I thought you might like this, to help your throat. Eat it quickly because it's melting," he said, and I immediately figured all was forgiven. It was perfect, just what I needed.

As I sat up and took the ice cream, Shrink suddenly sat up too, right in front of me, and before I could say anything, Sammy also jumped up, quicker than I even knew he could. He came over to me, sitting right alongside Shrink, both staring at me as if I were the teacher and they were the pupils with ice cream as the lesson.

66

I took a huge mouthful and it was perfect. It was the best ice cream I could ever recall having, perfect for my aching throat. I was later told they called it Snow Cream there, and it is pure white, full of sugar and little other taste, perhaps mild spice, but it was wonderful, and from that moment on a firm favourite of mine. I could tell it must have also been a favourite of both dogs too because they sat right to attention, not even daring to blink in case they missed something.

It was then that was the first time I found out that Sammy had a terribly habit of drooling when he saw food and wanted some of it. Not a little, but loads. "Oh Sammy," mum said. He looked at her quickly, then back to me, mildly aggravated at the interruption to his viewing pleasure.

I just laughed, but to stop him I prodded my index finger into the cream, scooped a little out and pushed it into his chops. I know, not the best of things to do, but I was a teenager, and didn't give much thought to such things. Immediately Sammy licked it all off, his eyes staring right at my finger as he licked it clean. That set Shrink off, and he stood up, almost hopping up, indignantly wondering where his was.

I scooped another small dollop of ice cream, giving it to him and once again Sammy began drooling all over, only this time onto Shrink's head! I just burst out laughing, immediately regretting it as my throat was so sore. Whatever that spider bite did to me it hurt and ended up with quite a bit of suffering. I wasn't entirely sure it was worth being bit to stay off school, given what I had to go through.

In the end I finished the ice cream, patted our two lovely dogs and they trotted off looking not the least bit disappointed they didn't have more.

I laid on the sofa a bit to relax, as I felt so tired from the illness. As soon as it got dark I went and got in bed and drifted off, not even bothering to put the light off.

I have no idea what time it was, but it was very dark, and the house was quiet when I woke up. My bedroom light was still on, and I couldn't hear anything. What most surprised me was that when I tried to kick my legs lower down the bed I got stuck. It was only when I lifted my head up that I noticed that Sammy had come into my bedroom, and honestly had the cheek to climb onto my bed, shift out his whole weight and plonk down right across it.

"Sammy, get down," I kind of whispered, mindful not to speak to loud mainly because it hurt, but also because I didn't want to bring my parents in. Given how warm it was I always kept my bedroom door open. We generally never kept the windows open, although every window had bars on them for security, the problem was mosquitoes. We did have to take a tablet every day which was Quinine, but even so bites were very unpleasant so apart from keeping windows open we also had a large metal hand pumped spray which we would spray repellent throughout the house.

Of course Sammy ignored me. He was like a canine house brick, large and heavy and with a similar unthinking mentality. I did find it funny, but it wasn't comfortable, so I tried pushing him. He was just too heavy and I wasn't up to it. His back was against the wall, so it wasn't as if I could shift him off sideways. I sat up and looked at him, and he never batted an eyelid, just carried on snorting like a grumpy old man. I bet he had never been so comfy as he was right there on my bed.

"Sammy, move," I prompted again, only this time nudging him with my foot under the covers. He let out the loudest sigh I have ever heard a dog offer, long and grumbling, part unhappiness at my annoying him and part expression of happiness at the lovely soft bed. It was only a single, no way big enough for both of us. Somebody had to go, and I increasingly had the feeling it was going to me.

In the end I slid sideways out of my bed and stood there on the cold tile flooring in my bare feet wondering what to do. As I stood there Shrink came wandering in, looking as if he had never been to sleep. He was a wonder that dog, nothing like any dog I have ever seen or had. You would think he had the mentality of a cat, but he was so changing with it, sometimes a loner and at other times so loving, as he knew how.

So here we were, Sammy laid out like a prince on his royal bed, and Shrink and I stood there as his humble followers. Shrink looked at the bed, then at me as if he really did understand what was going on. I just kept giggling, because big Sammy was funny, but the look on Shrink's face was priceless.

That was it, I was tired and gave in. I ached too much to argue, so just grabbed a pillow and walked out, to the living room, dropped the pillow on the sofa and laid down. Often at night in Kenya it would get quite cold, depending on the time of year. Monsoon season was particularly bad, when it would be a decided chill, but mostly it was fine to sleep without covers, and this was one of those times, thankfully.

I just zonked out and fell asleep. It was fine, but clearly a sign that I wasn't thinking clearly, given what I had just done.

"What are you doing?" a voice asked, waking me abruptly. I kind of jumped, opening my eyes quickly as if I had deep down been expecting it. I hadn't consciously thought about it, but it must have been there at the back of my mind because I knew what whoever it was meant straight away.

"Well I was sleeping," I half said, my mouth still coming to terms with the rest of me being awake.

It was mum who had found me. I could see it was still only early dawn. I figured she was checking on me due to being ill and I wasn't in bed she came looking.

"I can see that, but why aren't you in your bed?" she asked.

"There was no room," I replied, reasonably I thought.

"Come on, get your pillow, back into bed." I did as I was told.

What I saw when I got there made me not only laugh, but I couldn't believe it. Sammy was still sprawled out on the bed, not having moved at all, though for some reason he was fully aware my mum was there and had opened his eyes, looking at her quite sheepishly. What got me was Shrink, he was curled up where my pillow had laid, not even bothering to open his eyes. They had made my bed their own, and that was that.

It was at the exact moment my dad woke up for work, Monday morning, and chose just then to come to my room to see what was going on. I'm sure he must have thought mum and I had gone mad when he saw both dogs like that. He never wanted either dog on the furniture in the living room, so when he saw them both on my bed I expected fireworks.

To my even greater surprise he just took one look, yawned and went back into their bedroom. They had a bathroom/ toilet as part of their bedroom, so never used the main one. Dad just went in there and began to get ready for work, not saying a single word. Mum looked at me as if to say, wait for it.

Mum was determined to have no messing though and I think Sammy knew it. The second she went to step forward, holding her hand out to do something, he sat up quicker than I thought he was capable of, and without any further ado made his way off the bed, almost collapsing into the floor. He looked at mum, realizing that wasn't going to be far enough and drifted away reluctantly back to the cold hard world of the living room rug.

Then she turned to Shrink, who was in no mind to care what anyone thought. He never even opened his eyes, but I still got the feeling he knew we were there, that we were watching him. Mum leaned over, put her hand on him and gave him a gentle shake. He continued to play the silent doggy. I found it all very amusing, even though I wanted to get in bed.

Her patience soon ran out and she just picked him up like he was a cuddly toy. It was funny because he immediately opened his eyes and looked at me, as if to admit he had been rumbled. Poor Shrink, but poor me.

As she held him in her arms, I dropped my pillow where he had been laid and pulled the covers back, before getting in. Mum left me to it, walking out, carrying Shrink in her arms. I turned over, fluffed the pillow and closed my eyes. Bliss. It was nice getting back into my lovely warm bed again.

I can't recall why, but I opened my eyes one last time, and unbelievably there was Shrink, stood right by the side of my bed, nearest to my head, looking at me like I was a pork chop or something.

"Go bed," I said, then realizing they didn't actually have beds. It hadn't occurred to me before then that it needed sorting. Shrink naturally ignored me.

I smiled at him, which he took as encouragement to get on my bed again. He walked a little towards the end of the bed, looking up as if he were going to jump on, kind of hunched down a little, and before I could deny him, he tried to leap at the bed. Instead of springing onto it gazelle like, his face scrunched into the soft side of it and he bounced off. Again I giggled, trying to suppress my laughter because I was happy to have him in there.

He looked back at me without the least hint of embarrassment. I wondered if he thought I was to blame for what had just happened.

Once again he took a single step back and leapt, front paws at the side of the bed, this time doing a bit better, as he clawed onto the hanging covers with his front paws, using his chin to rest on the top of the bed. His little back legs were dangling there, waving around as if he were air dancing. No way could I stop myself from laughing, so I buried my face in my pillow and burst out laughing. I never knew dogs could be so funny. He was perfectly silly, so often, it was as if he was doing it deliberately.

I had tears in my eyes, just laughing to myself so much. It was a great show. Bit by bit he clawed himself up, more and more, as I watched. I felt the urge to help him, but then I would have been complicit in his dastardly deed, climbing up and back onto my bed, the forbidden area for dogs.

Finally Shrink did it, managing to top the mountain, well, get on my bed, and he took one look at me before circling near the bottom of the bed and dropping down into a little bundle of fur, his face hidden, perhaps hoping if we couldn't see his face then no one would know he was there.

I drifted off to sleep, and I think enjoyed one of the happiest sleeps of my life.

CHAPTER EIGHT

When I finally woke up I was alone, no sign of Shrink. It wasn't the pleasant awakening I had hoped for. My aches had eased, and the lumpy blotches on my skin seemed to have improved, as far as I could tell. The problem was my nose was itchy. Little did I know it was the beginning of something I would come to dislike intensely.

I sneezed, loudly. Mum came down the hall upon hearing I was awake.

"How are you feeling?" she asked. I nodded at her, but before I could answer he properly I sneezed again, now with a runny nose.

"Hold on, I'll go get you some tissue," mum said. I sat up, realizing I had to do something.

It turned out it was midday and very warm. I felt pretty good, but just couldn't stop sneezing. I got my dressing gown on, went into the dining room and sat on a chair. All the while mum was feeding me tissues. Whatever had caused it died down, and eventually went away.

"So you slept better then?" mum asked. I nodded.

"Hungry?" she asked. Again I nodded.

"Cat dog your tongue?" she asked and I shook my head.

"Dog's got it," I said and we both laughed.

Once that was over I went and sat back in the living room. Sammy was in the garden laid on the grass. Shrink was on the rug. As I sat down I picked him up, being small enough I could manage that much. I looked at him, gave him a quick hug to say thanks for the fun earlier. As soon as I did that, Sammy seemed to somehow notice the affection and for some unusual reason wanted in on it. He had never done it before, which was why I was so surprised. He came bounding in, displaying the kind of energy I'd never seem from him before, and rushed right up to me, actually standing on my foot. He was panting like a tractor engine, looking at me as if I had a bowl of food ready for him. Sadly, I didn't.

"Hello Sammy, would you like a hug?" I asked cheerfully, and to my joy it seemed yes he did. He nudged me a little closer, and I leaned in to him, wrapping my arms around him. He was so warm after being out in the sun, with that fluffy doggy smell, where his fur seemed to have a life of its own. It was a sweet moment, as we just kind of bonded for a moment.

That was the last time I was able to hug him like that, because as I sat back up again, I gave out the loudest sneeze imaginable. I rubbed my nose as it itched worse than ever, my eyes beginning to stream with tears. I sneezed again, twice quickly in succession.

"Now what?" mum asked. She was stood near the kitchen door, holding a glass she had just washed, drying it. I shook my head, but couldn't express anything, I was just so badly bunged up. It was awful. Whether I knew deep down or not what was wrong, I didn't even want to contemplate it.

Mum walked over to me, looking at me closely. She took a hold of one of my hands, immediately making the decision for me as to what was up.

Holding up my hand, she pointed at it. "Look, your hands are covered in dog fur," she explained. It never fully sank in with me what she might have meant.

"It could be Hay Fever, which would be a serious problem, given how dry and hot it is most of the time. If you get that, then you could be sneezing constantly."

As soon as she said it I disliked the idea, not being able to go outside without sneezing. She wasn't quite finished.

"But, given you have fur all over you," she began- then it hit me. She didn't even need to say it.

"The dogs, I might be allergic to them?" I asked, wide eyed and upset by the idea. We had only just got started, and here I was sneezing over them. Mum just nodded.

I got up and went into the bathroom, washing and rubbing the fur off myself. By the time I had finished, the floor looked all black, there was so much that had been on me. I rubbed myself clean with the towel, and looked in the mirror, only I didn't recognise who was looking back at me, red bloodshot eyes, last remnants of yellowed blotches, and hair a wild mess. It looked like I had been run over by a Rhino and left for the Vultures.

As if he sensed something, when I sat down again on the sofa, Sammy came up to me again. I instinctively went to put my hands on him, and was going to give him a hug when mum put her hand out. I felt awful, like I was going to be infected by them and had to stay away. I had it in the back of my mind that if I got bad enough they might have to go. Well, either they would or I would.

"It doesn't matter, wait til your dad gets in, and he might be able to think of something," mum said. I just pinned my hopes on that and waited.

"Are you hungry?" she asked, which for the first time in an age I realized I was. It was a clear sign I was getting over the spider bite, but also left me feeling at least some comfort that maybe it wasn't so bad.

Mum returned with some of my favourite food, cheese sandwiches. No matter what else went on, I always loved those. She placed the plate on the arm of the sofa and a bottle of pop on the small table at the side. Before I ate, I realized I needed the bathroom, so up I got and went. Looking forward to my sandwiches, hopeful that we could figure out the Hay Fever, or dog allergy, I did feel much better, at least until I got back to the living room. At first I couldn't figure out what it was, but I knew something was different, just not what.

I went and sat on the sofa, went to get hold of a sandwich, only to see an empty plate. What stood out, wasn't that it was empty, but that Sammy was sat across from me, looking very prim and proper, but he was busy munching on a thick cheese sandwich. Before I could react and sat anything to him, or even grab it, I spotted Shrink, laid on the rug, close to the fireplace, actually nibbling on the other sandwich. Not only had they stolen my food, but they had somehow figured out to have one each.

Shrink had the audacity to look up at me, blink once, and immediately get back to his meal. I didn't know whether to laugh or cry, but wasn't sure if I should say anything, because with this allergy, the last thing I wanted was for my parents thinking the dogs were food hogs, which they were, and that me being allergic to them, we should perhaps get a cat instead. Thankfully, we never saw hardly any cats in Kenya, big or small, which was fine by me.

Mum came to the top of the steps over the living room and looked at me. "Were they alright then?" she asked. I was crying out to say no, the dogs pinched them and I'm still hungry, but I was so torn over it I kept quiet about it.

"Oh yeah, they were lovely, thanks," I said. I actually thought about trying to grab back a little of what was left of Shrink's bit, but before I could even do that Sammy began vacuuming bits up, slobbering all over the rug, annoying Shrink too I think. It just wasn't meant to be.

Mum then came into the living room with her own food on a large plate. She had an apple, a banana and a couple of sandwiches of her own.

"Hey, I wouldn't mind a banana," I said and she handed me hers. Both dogs looked at me as if I were just there to hand them my food, but they got none of it. Greedy hounds.

I sat there taking my own good time eating it, nice and slowly, seeing how they liked being the hungry ones and someone else enjoying food for a change. Of course Sammy began the waterworks with his drooling, and Shrink began to look like he had swallowed a spring, bouncing around, tail wagging as if he really thought he would get some. He never did.

"Oh look, Sammy, oh," mum said in between mouthfuls of sandwich. "Go get them a bone each," she insisted, which ended my intent to pay them back, because they had just eaten my meal and now they were having a bone as a reward. Worse still, I couldn't say anything about it. Life can be so unfair at times, even when you're trying to be nice.

I stood up and got them a bone each. I was minded to nibble on them just to make a point. I might be daft, but I'm not that daft.

That settled it for the time being, but it surely wasn't the last of it. It was a lesson for how greedy and hungry they both were, which I would find out more of in time to come.

Dad walked in just as I was finishing my drink and mum her food. Both dogs were relishing their bones, and it was all quiet. He took one look at me, and declared, "Well you look better, school tomorrow then."

That was the last thing I needed. Bloodshot red eyes, blotchy skin and needing a shower. I felt awful, but when dad got an idea into his head, there was no changing his mind. I just ignored him.

"He's got Hay Fever, though it could be allergy to dogs," mum said.

"No, I'm fine," I insisted, before anyone could make something of it.

"Right, well, we will have to..."

I refused to wait for it, no way was he going to kick our lovely dogs out. "I'm completely fine," I shouted a little too loudly, as at the exact same time he said, "We'll have to go the chemists for some antihistamine." It kind of deflated me, yet again, and more proof that I should look before I leap.

"What are you shouting about?" dad asked.

"Why are you shouting?" mum asked.

I looked at them sheepishly, shrugging my shoulders. I didn't say anything, just waited, hoping they would let it go. Wisely, they did.

While Sammy and Shrink both went about their bone business, we set out into Nairobi. The chemist we went to was an Asian gentleman, and unlike in many countries he seemed able to prescribe pills and tablets that normally would only be available from a doctor. I ended up with several yellow tablets, which when I took one almost knocked me clean out, it was so strong. It stopped the allergy, but me too!

When we got back both dogs were slumped over, on the rug, no signs of any bones left. I could imagine being a dog, how it must feel, at the mercy of others in your life, but if you got good owners then life could be pretty good.

I ended up having a shower and by time I had finished, I looked much better, felt much better, and really sleepy. The tablets stopped me sneezing, but I felt like Sleeping Beauty on them.

I went to my bed, thinking I just couldn't keep my eyes open and as I laid down, who would peek his head around but Shrink. He stopped short of coming in, always with that hesitant look about him. He just waited, not blinking, just stared at me, but his eyes seemed to have something about them, like he knew me, and was always thinking about things. At times he could be playful, and others he could act as if he weren't even there. Maybe life had made him like that, where he had to switch off to it all, but deep down I could see what a clever little dog he was, and I ended up loving him as much as I have for any since. If anything ever sparked my love of dogs, it was him, with his cute little ways that at times seemed so human.

I laid on my side, head on pillow, feeling drowsy and bunged up. The last thing I recall was Shrink padding over on the hard tiles, before jumping up onto my bed. I had no way to be sure, but he seemed to know not to get too close to my pillow, perhaps instinctively, because he moved to the back, near the wall which the side of my bed was pressed against, and laid at the back of my legs. All I could feel was him snuggling down with me, just as the lights went out and I drifted off into a dreamless sleep. I suspect the same might well have been true of Shrink too.

CHAPTER NINE

It was a hard awakening the next morning. It was still early and pretty cloudy out, but light enough to see. It even felt decidedly chilly for the first time since I had gone to live in Africa. I had a blanket over me, but was otherwise still dressed in my t-shirt and shorts. My dad was stood over me, looking down at me.

"Morning," he said, quietly, as if he didn't want to disturb the house. I noticed Shrink still laid on my bed, but dad never said a word. Shrink was laid right alongside me, still fast asleep, oblivious to what was going on.

"Morning," I replied, still feeling sleepy.

"How do you feel?" he asked. I knew what he meant, he was asking if I felt up for school. It had been weeks and I hadn't been to school in so long, I'm sure my parents were aware that I needed to study. I felt like saying still ill, but truth be told I was ready to get out, and as much as anything wanted to meet someone new.

"Not bad, I feel better now," I replied, not even feeling the need to sneeze.

"Ready for school then?" he asked, but if I had said no at that point I think he would still have taken me. I just nodded and readied to get up.

"Great," he said, turned to leave. "I'll just go get your uniform," he continued. That word struck horror into my heart: uniform. I barely registered what it looked like after all that time, and all sorts of visions flashed before my eyes of white stripes and blue ribbons.

After a moment, he returned holding a hanger with it attached. It was comprised of a khaki shirt, short sleeved, which seemed a little clichéd, but not too bad, but worst of all were khaki shorts, not short ones, but just above the knee. They looked awful. My only saving grace was that every other boy in the school wore the same thing, though I quickly found out that most had better fitting shorts, and in that respect I really did stand out.

I'll never forget that morning of being dressed, getting into the car and seeing Sammy and Shrink at the front of the house, watching me leave. I wondered if they understood that I was coming back soon, but until I did they just seemed so sad. It was most likely just me that was sad, even if saying goodbye for only a few hours, but still it was hard. They never moved, just stood there, side by side, looking at me, wishing me goodbye. It was pretty tough, but nothing compared to what would come later. At least I knew I would see them again very shortly.

School was much like any other, wearing another silly uniform, to enhance discipline so it was and always is said, more like to keep us all the same and in check I would say. It was like most places I had been to, just getting through the day, but the best thing about my first day was meeting another boy who had also not long been in the country, and even better, lived near to me. It was the best possible outcome. His father was a teacher, much like the other young boys that lived down the street from us, but hopefully nicer. This boy was Yugoslavian, his name Sasha, and he too was a similar age to me, around fourteen. After some time talking to him I agree that after school we would meet up and do something.

The end of the day couldn't come soon enough, so when my dad finally picked me up I must have seemed excited.

"Looks like you really enjoyed today then?" he asked. I was immediately confused, how anyone could think a day at school could be exciting.

"Er, no," I said, pulling a face.

"Well you seem pretty upbeat," he replied.

"Oh, no, well I'm looking forward to seeing the dogs, and I met someone who I can spend some time with," I explained, finally agreeing I was pretty upbeat about it, just not what he was on about.

"Happy to see me and mum too I guess," he said.

"Oh yeah, sure," I said, drifting off into my own little world, planning ahead.

At the time there were no such things as mobile phones, and even landlines were a problem in Kenya, so communication was difficult if not in person. I had kept Sasha's address, and would call on him the moment I got back. After I had changed clothes of course.

The moment we pulled up at the house, it seemed as if not one thing had changed in the time since I left, that time had stood still. I was amazed to see both Sammy and Shrink stood outside the front of the house, looking at us as we drove in. Both dogs began to wag their tails, Sammy as best he could, panting in the heat, Shrink wagging so much his bottom shook so much I thought he was going to fall over.

I looked at my dad, wondering if he was thinking the same thing I was. "Do you think they've been stood there all day?" I asked, and really meant it. I don't think I could recall seeing my dad laugh that much. He ended up with tears in his eyes over it. I didn't ask why, but figured maybe I was wrong.

I got out, and the moment I did they both sprang over to me. OK, so Sammy didn't exactly spring, but it was his version of it, actually coming straight over to me. He just lapped up the attention and regardless of the allergy, I wanted to say hello and I did, giving him a big hard hug. He kept licking my bare arms, which was a bit soggy, but so loving and nice anyway. Shrink could barely contain himself, giving out little yelps. I ended up sat on the floor as he jumped on me, not knowing what to do with himself, I'd never seen a dog so excited, but I figured if he or both of them were like it every day I came back it was sure going to be fun.

I went in, said quick hello to mum. "Hi, how was your first day in?" she asked, but before I had a chance to say anything I went off down the hall to get changed. As good as anything that day, getting out of that silly uniform was the best thing.

Mum stood at the end of the hall, near the kitchen when I came back down, all changed. "So, how was it?" she asked.

"I met a lad, lives near here, I'm gonna go his and do something," was all I said.

"Right mum said, and before she could say another word I had the front door open.

"Oh, I want to take the dogs with me, he loves dogs," I said, looking for the rope. Dad came out of the kitchen, holding some collars and proper leads.

"Oh, yes," I said, amazed at how he had read my mind.

Dad handed them to me, but before I could go he blocked my getting to the dogs. "Before you go, I don't think you should take Sammy out, might be a bit too hot for him," he said.

I was obviously very disappointed, I had been thinking a lot about taking them both out, even if Shrink had been washed away in a tidal wave. Being a typical teenager, I forgot about that ten minutes after it happened.

There was no chance of me changing his mind, so I focused on putting their collars on. Both were blue and made of leather. I put Sammy's on, which was very large, and fitted him perfectly. I have no idea if he had ever had a collar on before, but he didn't complain about it, so it was fine. Next up I went to put Shrink's collar on, which was quite small, but he had such a skinny neck, even on the last hole when he put it on, every time he leaned his head down to the ground it fell off. I laughed every time it did, at which he would look up at me as if to wonder what was so amusing. I wonder if he ever knew that he was so funny. All he needed was a red nose and he would be the perfect clown dog.

Dad took hold of the collar and went back into the kitchen. He came out holding it tightly, looking down at it intently as he tried to prod a silver spike through it. After some tussling and plenty of effort, he managed to make two more holes, much closer in. I tried once again, placing it over Shrink as he stood looking up at me, showing all the trust in the world. I never failed to noticed such things, because for the first time with a dog I could instinctively feel something from him, something more personal and natural.

Shrink looked fine, with his perfect new collar, looking as if it were a suit of armour and he could take on the world.

I clipped on the rigid new lead and then looked up. "Right, we're off, hopefully a better time than last," I said, figuring I would deflate the elephant in the room before it had a chance to rampage over us. Dad smirked at my comment, but mum was not pleased.

"Make sure you come back safe, and don't be out long," she said looking at me as if I were going on a school trip and had to remember my packed lunch. Later on I would come to appreciate the difficulties in seeing children grow into young adults, managing their desires to grow and learn, while managing risks around us.

I was pleased to see Shrink looking so happy. I thought he would be the one to rebel against his collar and lead, but far from it, he positively bounced along out of the door and up the drive. He looked like a show pony trotting off, for the moment forgetting he was a dog. Once out of the gate he acted differently again, strangely acting all dog like, which of course wasn't strange for being a dog, but was different for him. He went and sniffed at some empty dirt outside, then ran up a little and sniffed a plant. Suddenly he had learned that dogs like to sniff. Before I could say anything to him, he lifted his leg against the plant, nonchalantly looking around, clearly enjoying himself.

Thankfully my new friend, Jason, lived up the road, rather than back down it, where we had last had problems. The road led right up to a junction which turned left to go further into more of the housing estate. To the right were some more houses where he lived, then further on to join the main highway that led to Nairobi city centre. I got to the top of the junction and looked around. When we had driven past in the car I hadn't really taken much notice, but being stood there, sort of alone, except for Shrink, who was sniffing around again, I really felt the chance to look out and see the place.

It always got dark early in Kenya, which was one of the reasons why drive in cinemas used to do so well, because you didn't have to be out late to go and see a film. I was mindful of that while out, because I knew I had to be back before dark. It wasn't so much that it was dangerous, just that mum would worry herself silly if I was out alone when dark, in Africa, as she kept reminding me.

I looked down to the left, seeing the houses sloping down in line with the hill, rows and rows of red slate tiled roofs, white walls and beyond huge trees, and all around varying plants such as dying yellow grass and banana plants here and there.

As I stood and looked, I noticed Shrink stood looking up at me. I could see how affectionate he was of me, just from the way he stared, and his eyes, so expectant. Every time I noticed him like that, I could see the intelligence in him, and how when he wanted he could connect with me, letting me know he was there, waiting for me to do something. At times he often seemed completely daft, but deep down I knew there was much more to him.

To the right the road went on endlessly, which I hadn't noticed before, because in a car you don't think about it, you just press go and off you travel, not getting out of breath, but missing so much. I began walking, almost heading into the sun. Of course it was dazzlingly bright, but not so much I couldn't stand it, I just loved the warmth on my skin, making me feel so relaxed. I wondered what Shrink thought of all the heat, but he just carried on, trotting along, panting with his little mouth open, acting as if it were another grand adventure. I realized in that moment just how much he trusted me, something I'll never forget, because at such a young age it's important to experience something like that, the responsibility that comes with it.

The houses grew sporadic the further I went, but I was looking for one that had a mail box outside, painted bright yellow. It was hard to make things out, and not easy because every time we got close to a large gate Shrink pulled away from me as if he thought it was ours and wanted to go in. Finally I did find what I was looking for. The place was a bit smaller than ours, but I knew it was the right one because the moment I got there I spotted Jason outside, sat on a kitchen chair, feet in a small plastic paddling pool, wading around and singing to himself. It was probably the strangest thing I had seen in Kenya, which was saying something.

Before I could get his attention two young boys went past me, clearly African, but they were wrapped up in their own little worlds. One had a long metal rigid wire, and when I looked down at the end I saw a box shaped metal thing, with what looked liked round wire wheels. He had gotten what seemed like metal wire coat hangers and shaped them into a small car, hollow frame, roundish wheels, and all attached to this wire stick which he used to move it along. I was amazed at his ingenuity, how he had created this minor toy, and how it worked. It struck me that his family may have been too poor to buy things such as plastic toys that I had taken for granted, and so he and others like him had to create their own. I'll never forget that. I was mesmerised by it, watching as these two boys jogged along, in bare feet, playing with this thing as if it were the most important thing in the world to them.

"What are you looking at?" a voice asked, making me jump. I turned around to look because Shrink had begun wagging his tale, so much that the both of us were shaking with it. Jason was stood at the gate, holding a poodle in his hands. I just burst out laughing, because he was the last person I would ever expect to be carrying a poodle. It was perfectly white and fluffy. I imagined it must have had daily baths to stay like that, because it got so dusty.

"Nice dog," I said, although I wasn't so cocky with him, because he was known to be something of a bully. Others didn't like him, because he was very full of himself. He and his parents were from America, and he loved his country, and made sure everyone knew it. To others it seemed to put them off, but not me, I liked him, and we got on well. He was nothing like how others seemed to think. He was taller than me, around the same age, but to look at him you would think he was much older. He was muscular and fair haired, very much the *all American*, and someone I quite admired, because he was so confident, and always bent on having fun. The poodle was just an anachronism. I had expected him to keep a tiger or something.

Shrink began yapping, looking at this fluffy poodle, forcing my friend's dog to hide under his arm.

"Ah, poochy woochy scared," Jason said and again I laughed even harder.

"What's so funny?" Jason asked, giving me a look which showed he appreciated the humour. I could see what kind of mood he was in, one that suggested he was in a mind to laugh with me as he punched me in the arm.

"Nothing," I said, calming down. I waited, expecting him to open up, but he didn't he rubbed his fluffy doggy and ignored me.

"What's his name?" I finally asked, trying to break the ice a bit more.

"Her. Her name is Fluffy," he replied, in all seriousness, still stroking her back and looking at her. I couldn't help myself, I had been thinking about him rubbing the fluffy little dog, and he was claiming her name really was Fluffy. What else could I do but laugh.

Jason looked up at me, with the kind of look which suggested he wasn't amused. If it wasn't for Shrink yapping constantly like he was I think he would have either walked off or had a go at me. I stopped laughing.

"Nice rat," he said, looking at Shrink.

"That's Shrink," I said.

"What kind of name is Shrink?" he asked. I thought to ask him what kind of name was Fluffy, but he no longer seemed in the mood to join in.

"Haven't you ever heard of Sammy Shrink, from the comics?" I asked, knowing he likely wouldn't have, but it showed I wasn't going to make fun any more.

"No, I read Spider Man and Superman comics," he said, which made sense.

I stood for a moment, looking at him, at Fluffy, around me, wondering what next.

"I guess you want to come in?" he asked finally, which was nice as I was roasting. I just nodded, deliberately exaggerated so that he couldn't miss it.

Finally Jason opened the gates and stood back. I walked in, as Shrink suddenly made a beeline for the pool. I accidentally let go of his lead, such was my shock at how much he wanted the pool.

"Hey, hold on," Jason began to shout, but before he could actually do anything about it Shrink ran quickly to the pool, jumped with all his might and landed in it with a huge splash. Water went everywhere. It wasn't a huge pool, about a foot high, about five feet around, but filled to the brim with nice cool water. Shrink seemed to see it as his to enjoy, wading around and splashing about like a baby in bathwater. Water went everywhere, as Jason and I stood watching.

"What's all the fuss?" a woman asked. I looked to the front of the small bungalow to see a white haired woman walking out. She seemed quite elderly and a little frail, but she was determined.

Jason looked at her, his face a picture of consternation. "Nan, his dog jumped into the pool," he said, sounding not at all like I had heard him before. He was no longer the leader type I had met, more like the young boy with his nanna.

"Oh hush, he's having fun," the lady said and I just smiled. She knew the truth, she was right.

"Hi," I said politely.

The lady looked at me, looked as if she were going to ignore me, but instead spoke. "Hello, you're English," she said, which kind of killed any conversation. I nodded in agreement, not sure how to react.

"Well I'm Nancy, his nan, and that's my dog he's holding," she said, making her way slowly to the pool. Shrink just splashed around for dear life, proving he was a water baby after all.

"Hi Nancy, I said, squinting because the sun had fallen to just the right level to catch me in the eye. She stood right next to the pool, watching Shrink have so much fun. I waited to see what she said, but I desperately wanted to take off my socks and shoes and dip my feet in, it looked so cool and inviting. We were all just stood there watching this little dog have all the fun, without a care in the world- it wasn't fair!

"Put her in," Nancy said, looking at Jason. I immediately knew she meant put fluffy in. I was pretty sure she wouldn't like it, but it was her dog, she would know best.

"You can't do that, she won't like it," Jason said, as if he could read my mind.

"Yeah, she'll be fine," Nancy said, and before anyone could react she grabbed hold of Fluffy and dropped her right in. I think Jason was more shocked about it than Fluffy was, but I just gasped, as I didn't really think she would do it.

Fluffy dropped in, made a huge splash which soaked us all, and splashed around as if seeking a quick exit. She padded her front paws, seemed to panic and then quickly realized she could touch the bottom of the pool. Just as she got to the edge of the pool, as if she were about to leap out, she stopped, looked up at Jason, as if to blame him for it, and then turned around to sniff Shrink, while he returned the favour.

"See, I told you she would like it," Nancy said, letting out a gravelly laugh. I decided not to wait around to see what happened next, I leaned over, rapidly pulled off my shoes and socks and stepped in.

"Hey, hold on," Jason tried to say, too late. "You can't put your smelly feet in there," Jason said, but by the time he had finished his sentence I had been stood there for ten seconds. He gave me the kind of look which suggested he was thinking of pushing me over, but Nancy slapped him on the arm. She seemed to know him so well.

In the end Jason just gave in and joined us, stepping back in, before sitting on his chair again, like the king of the pool. I thought about sitting down, but decided against due to his feet being in there, and two dogs doing who knew what to the water.

Fluffy and Shrink seemed to hit it off really well, like a house on fire. She was an all American canine, very well bred, and so nicely kept, and Shrink looked like a half rodent half dog, all black and looking very much like I would have imagined a dog from Africa looking. I had no idea what that meant, but to me he epitomised an image of an African dog. I wouldn't have swapped him for any dog in the world.

The sun eventually began to dip over the hills and I could see it was time for me to get going. "I'll have to go home," I said to Jason.

"You've only just got here haven't you?" Nancy asked.

"Yeah, but it's getting dark, I have to be in before then," I replied.

"Well his dad could drop you back in his car."

"He won't be in til nine tonight," Jason said.

"No I'll have to be home before then or mum and dad will come looking for me."

"Oh right," Nancy said. It was a kind gesture of hers, showing what a nice lady she was.

"Well Jason, you can walk him back," she insisted, which seemed like a good idea to me, but I knew he wouldn't want to. We were kind of friends, but I understood only so far. School friends, not best friends or anything like it.

"Nan, it's not far, he can go by himself."

"No, you'll go with him," she insisted. In a way I was glad, but it wouldn't have mattered if I had needed to go alone. In hindsight if I had know what was to come next, I would certainly have left by myself.

"OK, but I'll go on my bike," Jason said. His nan didn't say a word, I guess just relieved she didn't have to argue to get him to go.

It caught my attention. I had wanted a bike since I arrived in Kenya, so I could go off cycling more. Others I had met all had them, I just seemed the odd one out. I doubted either Sammy or Shrink would have wanted to go along with me though, neither of them had any chance of keeping up.

Jason turned to me and said, "I know a short cut," before going for his bike. I clapped my hands at Shrink, beckoning him from the pool. He was having a whale of a time, but I knew we had to go, time was getting short. It never took long for the sun to drop down and disappear, and I really wanted to get moving. Jason's nan kindly brought out a towel for me to dry on, and I quickly dried and put on my socks and shoes.

Jason came from behind the small house, having changed, pushing his bike. It looked pretty smart, but it occurred to me to wonder if he might just up and ride off on me.

"Right you two, hurry up and get going, and Jason you get back quickly," Nancy said. She was a lovely person, quite the opposite in some ways to Jason.

Without saying anything, Jason pushed his bike out of the gates as I followed. The moment we were outside he sat on his bike and began slowly riding. Instead of going back left, towards my house, he went right.

"Isn't the road to mine that way?" I asked. I knew the answer, but I was being polite, which often was a mistake with Jason.

"No, I know a short cut."

Shrink was back on his lead, but every few yards he kept stopping to shake. I had to stand back as he unleashed a blizzard of water everywhere. Each time he stopped to look at me as if waiting for me to pat him for being such a good dog. Each time he got the same response, me raising my voice to call him closer.

"Are you sure?" I asked, not believing him for one moment. I was in two minds to walk off the other way, but if I did he might not talk to me again, which I didn't want to happen.

He just nodded at me and turned to cycle away. I reluctantly followed, but from the way Shrink was dragging along I got the feeling he sensed what I was thinking.

We walked so far, turned down a small mud road, which led to a field. It looked quite large, untended, but green enough.

"You cross this field, then at the far corner, cut through a small gap between those houses, and it brings you out onto your road," Jason said. I just watched as he pointed. I wasn't entirely sure of going, but the sun was just tipping across the horizon and I was desperate to get in before it went altogether. If I went back the other way I just knew he wouldn't go with me, but it was too late to do anything about it.

"OK," I said quietly.

"Great," Jason said, sitting quickly onto his bike and riding away.

"Hey, hold on," I shouted." Jason just laughed loudly, cycling ever faster away until he disappeared round the corner. Off he went, and with it our friendship.

I felt awful, angry and upset. I knew I would just have to go for it, but I had a terrible feeling. Shrink straight away showed his feelings, as I began to walk onto the field, he tried to pull away from me, trying not to be dragged in. At one point it looked like he was going to pull himself off his collar. I was afraid if he got off his lead he might run away and I wouldn't see him again. It was bizarre, but it was getting darker by the second and I had no choice, I had to go. So I bent over and picked him up. He squirmed a bit, but settled in my arms. He might have been quite a little dog but he was certainly feisty when he wanted to be, not to mention quite heavy to carry. Regardless, I figured I had no choice.

I got about ten feet before I realized what I had gotten into, as I could hear the ground underneath my feet squelch. It wasn't a field, more of a watery bog, and who knew what lurked there. I genuinely felt like crying, but I knew I couldn't turn back, I had gone too far by then. Night finally descended upon me, and it was pretty much pitch black. One of the things about living in Africa is the lack of light pollution. When lights go off, it is so dark you cannot see a thing, so I was surrounded by utter darkness. All I could see were a single row of street lights ahead, off in the far corner. It was the only thing that gave me any hope that I might survive it.

So off I continued, slowly, one step at a time, carrying this little bundle of weight, terrified of what I might step on.

I got around halfway towards this light in the corner before my shoes filled with water. I struggled not to fall over in the rough, boggy ground. The only way I kept going was to say things to Shrink, in an effort to comfort him, but in reality comforting myself. Each time I said something his tail would wag for a second and stop, and then I could try again, all the while keeping on walking.

Around halfway across, I suddenly heard a noise. I thought at first I had heard water splashing and kept thinking I was suddenly going to fall into a huge pit of water. I walked a bit more, but then there it was again, this sound, only a little louder. I had all these odd things running round my mind about what it might be, thinking a giant lion was going to jump on me any second. Of course it was foolish, as if a lion would want scrawny little me.

I walked another step, and there it was again, only then it sounded much clearer. It was a distinct hissing sound. I felt ice in my veins, truly horrified as the thought trickled into my mind that there was a snake nearby. I had been concerned for spiders or something similar, but it never occurred to me until then that I might get close to an actual dangerous snake. Nobody had told me about them!

I just stood there feeling so angry and scared, not wanting to walk another step because each time I did I felt that I was going closer to something that might hurt me. I was so angry about Jason, that he had done this to me. I just never had much luck since going there with friends. The adults all seemed to nice to me, and us as a family, all so happy and positive, regardless of their surroundings, but young people, well maybe they were bored, but things were always difficult.

There I was in the pitch black, holding onto this little dog, feet soaking wet with the boggy watery grass, beginning to shiver with the cold, holding a little dog that I was afraid would get hurt more than I would if I let him down. I was stuck.

Before I could decide what to do, Shrink began wriggling so much I couldn't contain him. He wriggled hard, shaking his back legs, until I had no choice but to let him down.

"Shrink!" I shouted loudly. He wouldn't listen to me. For a moment I could see his dark outline against the ground, like a moving shadow, then I heard a yapping sound in the distance. "Shrink," I called again, and really felt like crying. In my mind he could have been fighting with anything. I waited, listening as much as I could, but all I could hear was my own heartbeat pounding away in my chest. It was awful, so much, so overwhelming that I genuinely felt sick.

I was cold, wet and alone. There was no signs of Shrink, but I knew I couldn't do anything about it. I had lost him. So I began to walk, and as I did so, I called out his name, clapping my hands. Each time I did I paused a second, listening again, but there was no sign of him. In my walks out with my dogs, things never went well. This proved to me I should resist the urge to do so again.

Things became so bad I just began to plod on, not worrying if anything happened to me. I was shaking still as afraid as ever, but I knew something had to happen, so I carried on, walking to what I had realized was a large orange sodium street light in the far corner.

It must have been around ten feet or so to the edge of the field when I almost fell over. I tripped on something, but my state of mind being so all over the place meant I couldn't immediately focus on what it was. I was close enough to the light by then that as I stared at it, I could see its thin body, winding around, lifeless, and quite green in colour. It was only small, not something that I might be afraid of if I had seen it in daylight, but then again, perhaps I was only kidding myself. I bent over, trying to get a better look, only to realize it was a snake. I almost jumped out of my skin, leaping back, away from it, shrieking so loud anyone would have thought I had been attacked by something savage.

I waited, staring at it intently, only it didn't move, no sound, nothing. I figured it was dead, eventually plucking up the courage to get a little closer. It was on its back, looking pretty yucky, but still I felt awful for what had happened to it. I stood up, took in a deep breath, and straight away saw Shrink stood there, looking up at me, as if he were wondering what I was looking at.

"Shrink!" I said again loudly. The moment I did his tail wagged like mad and he bounded over to me. I picked him up, hugging him. I have no idea if I was lucky, or if he was, or if being born in Africa meant he knew how to look after himself. If that were true, it may well have been that he helped me more than I'll ever know.

No matter what, there was no way I was going to let him get down again. I just trotted off, almost running, him bouncing in my arms, desperate to get off the field. The corner of it opened out into a small gap between two houses, leading through a dirt track, and back out onto the road near the bottom, where I had gone before, with the broken drain and Shrink's last adventure. I got onto the road and headed back up as quickly as I could, finally getting to the large black gates. As soon as I walked up to them I could see mum stood there, and further beyond my dad walking off up the road.

93

"He's here," mum called, thankfully catching his attention. I let Shrink down to the ground and he ran in, lead trailing off on the tarmac.

"Where have you been?" mum demanded, but straight away she could see I was upset, and let it be.

Dad came back down, looking at me the whole time. Often he would be angry, but it was good that this time he waited, wanting to hear what I had to say.

"Jason told me to go this short cut, across that field, but then left me to it, and it turned out to be a boggy marsh, full of all sorts," I said. I was never one to go telling tales, but this was serious, I could have ended up in a terrible way.

Dad looked at me, clearly angry. "Well you won't be going to his again, and he won't be coming here either," he said.

"No, not if he's going to do that," mum agreed.

I was very undecided over whether to tell them about the snake, but I could see mum was already frantic with worry, so didn't. It was many years later that I told her about it, which caused quite a shock, but thankfully Shrink seemed to have saved me. To this day I will always be thankful for him being there.

CHAPTER TEN

Things felt quite different for me after that night. I never really felt so safe again, not quite seeing things the same at all. Obviously my parents had no idea why, but it was never discussed. I got into life in school as best I could, but I still missed home, and all my friends from there too. Once the initial surprise and wonder of being in a new country settled, I began to notice more and more how we lacked a lot of what we had from home, the very least being things to watch on television. Even the newspapers if we could get them were a day out of date, and at the time with no Internet, hardly any telephones and my not being able to drive, I began to get itchy feet, wanting more.

Though neither said anything to me, I could tell they felt the same. Dad was doing alright in his job, but mum was clearly bored at home all the time. She would read books endlessly, and that caught me too, which is where I developed my love of reading, long before writing was ever an idea.

Quite out of the blue, an idea occurred to me, and I just blurted it out. "Could we maybe go back the England, for a holiday, to see people?" I asked. My sister had stayed there, as she had her own life and didn't want the disruption.

I had said it to both of them, but mainly it was to dad, because he made those kind of decisions at the time. The moment I said it Sammy came wandering up the few steps from the living room, breathing heavily, as was his way. In order to break the silence, I just knelt down, putting my arms around him, hugging him. He stood there, grumbling in his own, old little way. I don't know if he understood the significance of our conversation, but he was always such a wise old dog, anything was possible with him.

"I wouldn't mind that," mum said. I could see from the reaction on dad's face that he wasn't quite seeing it as a need to go for a quick holiday. We had been there quite some time, settled in, in some ways, but things were not quite as we had expected. Whether he had known that for some time I had no idea, but if he did, he never said.

"I guess you could do that," he said, at which I looked at mum and we smiled at each other. I always enjoyed flying, but the moment I thought of it I looked at Sammy, and realised how much I was going to miss him, and Shrink, even if it was going to be a couple of weeks.

"When though, when should we go back?" mum asked.

"I can't go, not with work, but you can. We'll have to get two tickets. I'll find out and let you know," dad said. I couldn't help but be excited to go back and tell everyone of my adventures, good and bad, but most of all about our two new dogs.

That discussion had taken place after tea, quite late on a Saturday night. Given how quickly it got dark in Kenya, we had gotten into the habit of going to bed early, and that's what happened that night. Mum and dad said goodnight and went off, and I went to my room. As I went off Sammy followed me, which was unusual because he usually headed straight for the sofa. I didn't really feel anything different, because I knew we were only going to a quick break and would be back again, but I suspected he might have had just such things happen so often in his life, people he had gotten to know leaving him, that he imagined not seeing us again. Of course I knew he was a dog, perhaps not really thinking so much, but I couldn't escape that thought, when not only did he follow me to my room, but he actually went to my bed, and climbed on it, like a fat horse climbing onto a set of hay. I couldn't stop laughing, but did so quietly, as he pushed his front legs on, then struggled to get his back legs on, trying to lift one leg up, trying again and again, but it was too high, then he would do the same with the other leg. He was such a funny dog.

In the end I just got a hold of his leg and lifted him, gently pushing his huge body onto my bed, and watched him shuffle up, then flop down on it, the bed bouncing as his heavy weight settled. He took one look at me, then flopped his head down, breathed out heavily, and to all intents, said goodnight. As much as I giggled, I knew I wasn't going to be able to fit into my bed because of him, but I didn't mind so much as that night it was very warm and I loved the idea of snuggling up beside him.

As I was about to get up and put the bedroom light off, Shrink suddenly appeared, his little nose poking gently around the door frame from the hallway. I watched intently, sitting on my bed, as he leaned in a little, so he could finally see us. I smiled at him, watching him move, his tail obviously wagging, but I couldn't see it as all the other lights were out.

I stood up and slowly walked towards him. Sammy just laid there, snoring away like an old tractor, he was well gone, no

chance of him getting up. I went over to Shrink, in reality
thinking there was no way he was getting on the bed too, as
then I would have to sleep on the floor, and it was cold tiles, no
way was I going to do that!

As I got to Shrink he quickly turned around and trotted off
down into the darkness in the hallway. I was mistaken thinking
he wanted to come in, it seemed like he was playing games. I
did think he was running to get his ball, but he never returned,
so eventually I followed, feeling curious.

I didn't put any lights on, as I didn't want to disturb my
parents, the clicking noise, and their door being open, so I
walked off into the darkness, trying to see, hoping not to trip
over him. I had visions of walking across the field, but didn't
want to be reminded of it any more by falling over him.

As I got to the top of the step to the living room, I could see
the windows and doors which led to the garden, curtains all still
wide open. Those windows and doors lined the entire wall,
being made up of small square panelled black painted metal,
and locked securely. What little light there was gave enough for
me to see the steps, and Shrink stood right by the black metal
door, facing outside.

As I quietly walked down, he continued to stare, ignoring
my approach. I walked up to him, peering out, wondering what
was going on.

I initially thought there might be an intruder, but as I looked
out I couldn't see anyone. I wondered if it might be an animal
of some sorts, but it was unlikely. It was then that I saw some
lights, right across, way beyond our back garden. The silence
was broken by some sounds, which to me seemed quite
mechanical, deliberate.

"What is it Shrink?" I asked him, and he turned to look at
me, then quickly back, eyeing what was going on outside.

Whatever it was intrigued me. I knew better really, but
couldn't resist opening the door to have a look. I turned the key
and pushed down on the handle, pulling the door open. Things
often evaded common sense with me, because I wouldn't think

about consequences. The moment I opened the door Shrink shot out, into the garden. I almost yelled at him, but my track record recently had been pretty poor, so bit my lip, instead following him out to try and grab him.

The air was unusually cold that night, the skies totally dark, no clouds, no light from anywhere, but what tranquillity there was, was broken by the sounds coming from across the way. I managed to catch sight of Shrink, stood at the picket fence, near the small gate. I think if he could he would have gone over the fence and down into the back garden to wherever the noise was coming from. He couldn't, thankfully, so he stood looking through the gap.

I slowly walked out towards him, feeling the chill air against my legs. Being so warm indoors I always wore pyjama shorts, but outside for the first time that late, I finally became aware of just how cold it could get in Africa, even in the warmest of periods. It was then also the first time that I thought of all those people who had so much less than us, and yet had to cope with a life like that. It was a lot to take in for a teenager.

I stood beside Shrink, beginning to shiver, but looking out, across the darkness. It was only then that I noticed just what lay beyond our big fence, and what Shrink had found so fascinating. Lights adorned all across the hilltops. I couldn't see exactly what they were, but they seemed like hundreds of fireflies, all flickering, except I could smell wood burning, and knew there was more to it.

The sounds I had heard weren't machines, but music, playing here and there, from radios, from people doing things themselves, though I couldn't see what. Some were just some singing, making their own music, their own life. What I was seeing was the small shanty town at the back of our home. It was such an anachronism, to see such haphazard life going on, right beside us, and in a way which was a world away from what we were used to.

I found it in some ways disturbing, but also magical, that they could live a life which I found harsh, and yet also so different to ours, and here they were living it on their own terms. It was difficult, but for me at that age, I could see something positive from it.

Never one shy of being foolish, I went quickly back into the living room, put on some shoes, got a jacket and wrapped it around myself, then quickly went back out. Shrink didn't move, but I imagine his thoughts if he were capable were far different than mine. Perhaps he might have recognised something there that he was used to. Of that I'll never know.

I opened the small back gate, knowing full well that there was a huge fence all around the back garden, so I didn't have to worry too much about Shrink. There were long winding concrete steps leading down the steep hill, to the area where there still remained so many vegetables like sweet potatoes and others. I carefully went down, as Shrink shot off again, running down and across to the large fence at the back. I followed him, intent on getting a better view for myself of what was going on.

The fence must had been all of ten feet tall, and perhaps more. It was so dark it was difficult to see, but that didn't stop me, or Shrink. As I got closer I could see him stood there, pacing sideways, trying to get a better view. I had a feeling if he had found a gap he would have run off, but there was none; I just knew it was alright.

I walked closer to the fence and looked up, to see there were struts going into the ground, large poles, fastened in with concrete. Alongside these were similar struts, made of wood, but thinner. I could see there were enough that I could climb onto them, and sufficient gaps in the fence that I could gain a hold onto the fence, enough that I could get a hold and climb up. So I did.

It was totally dark on my side, so I climbed up, believing no one could see me. Shrink came and stood right beneath where I was climbing, as if he believed he would be able to follow. When he realized he wouldn't he just stood looking at me, as if I were ascending to the clouds, quite by magic.

I finally got enough traction that I could lift myself to the top of the fence, so my head was sticking over, my hands placed atop the rugged fence, my feet on a horizontal slat of wood, that I would be comfortable, and see, without fear of falling.

It still needed time for my eyes to adjust, but within seconds I could see vague movement around there, outside, in what seemed to me to be an alien world, something far removed from anything I could have imagined Africa to be. The shadows that moved were people, moving around, going about their business, aside so many small shacks and huts, they went as far as the eye could see, across and away, and sideways into the distance.

As my eyes became accustomed to it all, I could see so many flickers of light, so many fires and flame lights, that it seemed an ocean of stuttering luminescence, with people blurring the reality of it. I wondered if what I saw wasn't real, that I was sick again, and in the blink of an eye I would wake up to find myself in my bed. That never happened. I could feel the soft air against my bare arms and face, but most of all there were a myriad of smells, all kinds of food cooking, sweetcorn, potatoes, some kind of meats, everything. I knew these people had next to nothing, but through their own hard work and ingenuity they had found a way to live, and survive even in these harsh conditions. A part of me wanted to feel awful for them, but they didn't deserve my pity, they got my respect, for what they achieved every day in life.

I laughed a little as I could hear Shrink sniffing. I looked to see his little nose poking through a tiny gap in the fence. He too had noticed the food being cooked.

There was no electric there, no running water, nothing that many would take for granted, just what they could get for themselves from what little there was. What they lacked for power they gained through fires, to cook, to keep warm, to see by, it was in some small way the essence of their lives.

A tall thin man walked past, not too close to the fence, dressed in some kind of all over cloth. He turned to looked at me, surprising me, that anyone could see me stood there behind the fence in the dark. He didn't stop, just looked, then turned away, moving on.

The smells were powerful and profound, so much burning wood, and yet that sense of taste that came from the food, it evoked a kind of connection with what they were doing, that it was a part of them.

Then a thump came from one of the nearby huts, and then another. I wondered if someone was going to bang and make a noise, to perhaps complain that I was intruding on them, that this was their place, and someone like me wasn't welcome. It never happened. A man cried out, not in pain, but in song, long and serious, before others joined in. It wasn't the whole community, just these few near, but some close by joined in, as a sound of an instrument that I couldn't see began playing. It was simple, just strings, but it sounded so impressive, that bonded well with their singing. A woman joined him, as others clapped their hands. I saw then what this brittle, broken community could do, what these people were capable, of. I felt something quite different to anything I had before.

Many say that when you live in Africa, it becomes a part of you, that when you live there and later leave, you never really do leave, and that a part of you remains there forever. I felt that, that I had become a part of this country, and that its memories and what I had been through in my time there had created a bond which would never be broken, either through memories, or feelings, or something more, something unspoken.

I jumped so much that I nearly fell off the fence when a young woman spoke to me. She was stood right beside the fence, and had moved so quietly, that I hadn't even noticed her arrival.

"Hello," she said, at which I almost panicked enough to want to run and leave. Thankfully I didn't, the pull of what I was seeing was too much.

"Hi," I struggled to say.

"Do you think I could have some of that food you have there, some of those potatoes?" she asked. I couldn't see her properly. She spoke such perfect English that I have never forgotten that moment.

I waited, thinking, wondering what to do. I thought to immediately say yes, to jump down to gather some for her. That was my first instinct. Then I wondered, if I did this for her, then what?

"I can't," I said, and the moment I said it, I regretted it. "If I give some to you, others will ask, and where do I stop, who do I say no to?" I asked. She nodded I could see, thanking me, before walking away.

It was something that has stuck with me to this day, wondering if I did the right thing. There were so many people there, so many who would need more, and yet there I was as a teenager, having to decide what was right or wrong in such a situation.

To this day I never forgot that moment, but more importantly, I never forgot how good those people were, because if they had wanted to they could easily have gone and stolen from the garden, and yet none ever did. It showed me something about the people of Africa, and their ability to stand up and be righteous, even when other circumstances were so difficult. It left me asking questions since, about what I did, and who I was, whether I should ever have the right to say no again, to someone in need of food.

So the last image I had was of a large range of people, some stood, some sitting, around fires here and there, clapping, singing, eating or drinking, and just being in a community of people, doing the best they could, and with it making the night quite amazing for me.

At the very least it gave me plenty to think about.

The air was growing cold, and Shrink I could tell was tired. He kept looking back, away, wanting to leave. It was the right moment, and so I jumped down, wiped my hands, walking back to the house. I closed the small gate, shut and locked the back door, and went back into my bedroom. Shrink didn't follow me that night. I have no idea why, but he stayed in the living room, perhaps knowing to leave me to my thoughts.

I got into bed as best I could, not too concerned that Shrink wasn't there, because I had this great huge lump of my other dog, Sammy to cuddle up to. Thankfully he left me a tiny bit of bed.

I didn't know, but that night would be a significant one for me, as things were about to change forever.

CHAPTER EVEVEN

The following morning, when I awoke I knew I had slept well. Well enough that is, with a huge dog laid next to me. Mum came in to wake me for school, only to find Sammy laid beside me. I was flat on my back, and he had shifted onto his tummy, enough that he had managed to rest his big head on me. He must have slept well too, because he was wide awake. We both looked at mum, he looked a little more sheepishly than I did. I just laughed about it. I thought for a moment to say something to her about what I had experienced the night before, but then it was another first, for the first time I didn't confide in her. It wasn't because I wanted to hide anything from her, just that for the moment it was something private, that I valued, and wanted to keep to myself.

Sammy yawned a great huge yawn, reminding me how bad his breath could be. It was tremendous, as if something had died in his mouth and he was bragging about it.

"Pooh, Sammy, please," I said to him, at which he took his cue and stood wearily up, before sliding off the bed, crushing me in the process.

"Your dad has gone early to work, he said he's got something to tell you when he gets home," mum said. I thought nothing of it, but just got up to get ready.

I went off to school, the day being mostly like any other, another glorious sunny day. Something did feel different though, my perception of the people around me was different. Especially after the night before. I didn't dwell on it.

Dad picked me up as usual, but when driving back he didn't say much to me. I was a bit tired, figured he was, and so left it at that.

When we got in he threw his car keys on the hall table, as always, and went to get a drink from the fridge.

"Do you want a drink?" he asked, and I nodded. He got us two bottles of fizzy pop, topped the caps on them and handed one to me.

Mum had been sitting in the living room, and had got up to come speak to us. I was past the stage of giving her a hug, at least until I grew up a bit more and realised how much I liked it, and that it wasn't daft.

Sammy, being the lazy type, would look at me, giving me a stare, which would be his way of excitedly saying hello, happy to see you. He couldn't even muster the energy to wag his tail, but I didn't blame him, it was just so hot.

Shrink was the opposite. If I didn't bend down to him, he would jump up on two hind legs and bounce, over and over, giving little yaps until I gave in. If I bent over to him, he would nip at me until I got lower, and then once down he did what he always did, what he did then, jumped on me, licking my face, going mad to show how much he had missed me. I always loved how he groaned at me, with his little tail wagging so hard. He seemed to be groaning that I had dared to stay away for too long.

"Right, well, sorry to have to say this, but I have something to tell you," dad said after swigging a mouth full of lemonade.

I was sat on the floor, and looked up at him. I had thought he meant mum, but he meant me.

"Why, what's up?" I asked innocently.

"Well, my contract here is up, and it isn't being renewed, so we're leaving," he said. It was the worst kind of bombshell, I felt sick in my stomach which until then I don't think I had ever experienced. For some reason I instinctively hugged Shrink closer and he seemed to nudge into me all the more.

"So what, are you going to get another job here?" I asked. It was odd, because before I had felt a little lost, that there wasn't enough television, no newspapers or magazines, no recent music charts, no proper friends. I couldn't connect at all, and then in such a short space of time, I had changed to the complete opposite. The single thread which kept challenging me then, the sole thought was, what about my dogs? I was too afraid to ask in case I gave life to the idea that they would suddenly disappear. I remained frozen to the spot, afraid of what I knew was inevitable.

"No, there are no jobs here for me now. We'll have to go back home," dad said. I suspected he knew it would be a problem for me, but not how much.

I just sat, looking down at the ground. I was torn, because I had grown to love Africa, but I also missed being back home, and all that my life offered before.

"What about the dogs? I asked. "My dogs."

Dad didn't say anything, but mum did. "I'm so sorry, but they can't go with us," she said. I think she was sensible enough to know there was nothing she could say that would make it better, so didn't try.

I just had no way to respond. Given I was a teenager, I didn't want to show any emotion, so tried to hide it as best I could. The first thing I did was to try to find something positive from it.

"When, do we have some time before?" I asked, struggling to speak without crying. It was awkward for me, because I was on the threshold of growing up, and yet still at the mercy of my emotions.

"No," dad said, which was like ice into me. "We'll have to pack, and I'll arrange plane tickets back home, possibly for this weekend.

If I had fainted there and then it wouldn't have been a shock to anyone. I still don't think he appreciated the impact it had on me. Going back for a break seemed a good idea, but forever, and without my wonderful dogs. I couldn't cope with it.

"Can't we take my dogs?" I asked, at which point I gave up trying, and emotion swept over me. I could feel tears in my eyes, like twin dams waiting to burst. My voice said it all, giving up any pretence at bravery.

"We can't, there's just no way," he said. He never showed too much emotion, but even then I think he knew it was serious for me. His answer was to brave it out, to be tough, and get it done with quickly.

Before I could say anything, try any form of pleading he finished what he had been planning. "I've spoken to one of the men who works at the factory, Tuo Mbeke, he said he will have them both. I've agreed to pay him for their upkeep, and he promised to keep in touch so we know they're alright.

It was a tiny crumb, not much, but it gave me something to cling onto. I knew full well no amount of arguing would change his mind, no matter what I said. Dad finished his drink, patted me on the shoulder, and apologised, before going for a shower.

"Can't we do something, we can't give them up?" I pleaded. Mum's face said it all. She had no answers, she wasn't in charge. She hugged me, and I burst into tears, hugging her back. It was one of the hardest moments of my young life, to go from such happiness and elation, to feeling so broken by it. There had been a lot of changes I had been through in Africa, but the impact of those dogs had the biggest on me, more than anything.

Dad came back, could see how upset I was, but there was little he could do. He never really seemed to know how to even try.

"We'll sort it quickly, so you're not hanging on," he said, and left it at that. I wanted to shout and scream, but it wouldn't do any good.

That night was a long one. I never ate any tea, and just sat looking lost. There wasn't much said by any of us. Every now and then I tried to hug one of the dogs, but I couldn't do it because I knew I would cry too much. It was too painful.

When we all went to bed, Sammy came and looked at me, and I got out of bed, kneeled down and hugged him then. I squeezed him so hard he burped! I laughed and cried some more. Shrink didn't come to me, I suspect he knew what was what. I tried twice to get him to come to me, but he wouldn't, he just peered around a corner, or stayed away.

It was a long night, and I didn't sleep until the early hours. When mum woke me I felt so sick, knowing what was coming. Without getting dressed I went out into the hall, to see dad stood there, both dogs on a leash, as he was about to go take them away. I took one look and cried so much I don't think I ever have since.

"Just give them a hug," mum said, and I could see she was crying too then. I just did it, wanting it to be over. Dad didn't wait around, he just went out the door and closed it. I went and sat on the sofa in the living room, continuing to cry, as mum tried to comfort me.

I didn't go back to school, there was no point by then. Besides I would have just been too sad for it. Mum and I spent the day packing what things we had. Most of the things weren't ours, but ornaments and mementos of our time there we put in suitcases, and packed our clothes.

By the time dad got back, it looked much like the time we had arrived. It all seemed like a strange dream, where we had only arrived for a holiday a few days before and were leaving again. The fact was we spent a year there, yet it flew by so quickly seemed very strange.

I never spoke to dad, and he didn't to me. It was done, and all I was left with were never ending regrets I hadn't said goodbye to my dogs properly.

"So when will we be flying out?" mum asked.

"Tomorrow, night time flight to Amsterdam, then back to London Heathrow, and train back after," he said. I couldn't believe how quickly it was all happening, but all I could think about was where were the dogs, what were they thinking now? I imagined Shrink would be missing me terribly.

Again I never ate, I sat for a while and then went to bed. During the following day dad tied up last minute things from work, then returned ready to pick us up to go to the airport.

"Here, this is Tuo's address. If you write to him, he has promised to keep in touch, to tell you how they're both doing," dad said. It offered me some comfort, but not a huge amount. I could feel better for knowing they were happy with someone dad trusted, but when I pictured their faces, I just felt lost again.

We put suitcases into the car and turned to take one last look at the place. It had been an amazing experience, but for me I knew I would never see this place again, the place I would call home. I was right, I never went back.

The drive was busy but quiet for us. I knew someone was picking the car up from the airport after we left. I never asked dad why his contract ended, and he never really said, preferring to look forwards only.

For my part I just wanted home by then, to get on the flight, and go home and pretend none of it ever happened.

It was a long uneventful flight. I just sat, not saying much. I was angry with mum and dad, that they didn't do more to try to bring them back, but I knew it was a lot of money, and he was no longer working, so figured enough out that I wouldn't have to be too angry and full of blame.

Getting back into London, to Heathrow was a shock in many ways, not least how cold it was. Going from such a warm climate, we had forgotten how cold it was for us mostly. We went into the terminal ready to find our bags.

I got out onto this great open concourse, with all these people, and just stood there, feeling so lost. It was ridiculous, I no longer felt at home in the country I had grown up in.

Mum stood by me, looking at me, lost herself for what to say. She could see I was so distressed, but she had no answers, and I think felt the same too.

Dad went and got our bags, before coming back over to us. Until that moment we hadn't spoken to each other at all, but then he stood right in front of me.

"I'm sorry," he said, which helped, at least to show he was human after all. I didn't say anything, but nodded a bit, to acknowledge he was thinking of me.

"I'm sorry I couldn't bring Sammy back, but the truth is he was too old, not just to fly, but to stay in quarantine for six months." I had forgotten that dogs going into the UK would have to sit in quarantine for six months, which was the time required to see if they showed any signs of illness or diseases. I just shrugged, because I knew he was right, but it still didn't help much.

"Tuo will send you updates on how he is, and how they are," mum said, and I appreciated her efforts to comfort me.

"However," dad said, at which he pulled out some papers. "Shrink, can go into quarantine, and is being taken there, and in six months, we will go and pick him up, and he will be coming to live with us. Forever," dad said proudly. To say my eyes lit up would be the biggest understatement of my life, but they did, and I breathed in so quickly and so heavily I thought I was going to faint.

"No way, really?" I asked, struggling to find something to say.

"Yep, for real," at which dad showed me his entry papers and paperwork for quarantine.

Mum laughed a little, looking at my dad. "Why didn't you tell me?" she asked, proving she had known nothing.

"We were so busy, and I wasn't sure if they would take him in, or if we could afford it. When I saw how upset you both were, I just thought go for it."

By then I was beaming, smiling so much, I could have done back flips. I still felt so sad for Sammy, but trusted Tuo to keep us updated in big lazy Sammy.

During the following months I kept a close eye on Shrink, as he spent his time waiting for release to us. I got several short notes about Sammy, often with not much to say, because he was never an active dog, but I knew he was loved and cared for and happy, and that was all that mattered.

Eventually Shrinks time came, and we all went together to get him. It was an amazing day. Being able to hug him felt wonderful, the little bundle of fur, his tail wagging so hard I thought it might fly off. We took him home, and once again settled into a new routine, which I knew meant he would never leave us again.

We never did move abroad again, which suited me fine, and Shrink too I think.

Sammy and Shrink both went on to live full and happy lives, and remained then and now, a constant reminder of my amazing time, living in Africa. For all the love and fun they gave us, I shall never ever forget, my two dogs in Africa.

Did you enjoy this book?

If you did, please consider leaving a review on the Amazon website. Good reviews encourage writers to write as well as helping to promote our creative works to others. Whether it is a few words or a few sentences, if you could spend a few moments of your time with this it would be much appreciated.

Thank you.

Real- life Photographs of events, characters and actual locations used for this novel are available for viewing, at **http://www.davidcowdall.com** *on the Two Dogs In Africa webpage.*

Made in the USA
Coppell, TX
07 November 2020

40945087R00061